She Writes

Love, Spaghetti and Other
Stories by Youngish Women

She Writes

Love, Spaghetti and Other
Stories by Youngish Women

Edited by Carolyn Foster

Second
Story
Press

National Library of Canada Cataloguing in Publication

She writes : love, spaghetti and other stories by youngish women / edited
by Carolyn Foster.

ISBN 1-896764-68-1

1. Short stories, Canadian (English)—Women authors. 2. Canadian fiction
(English)—21st century. 3. Canadian fiction (English)—Women authors.
I. Foster, Carolyn (Carolyn S.)

PS8321.S52 2002   C813'.01089287   C2002-903669-0
PR9197.33.W65S5 2002

Copyedited by Andrea Knight
Cover design by Margie Adam, ArtWork, Toronto
Text design by Jennifer Tiberio

One Tin Soldier
Words and Music by Dennis Lambert, Brian Potter
©Copyright 1969 Universal – Duchess Music Corporation (BMI)
International Copyright Secured All Rights Reserved

*Second Story Press gratefully acknowledges the support of the Ontario Arts Council
and the Canada Council for the Arts for our publishing program. We acknowledge
the financial support of the Government of Canada through the Book Publishing
Industry Development Program, and the Government of Ontario through the Tax
Credit Program.*

ONTARIO ARTS COUNCIL
CONSEIL DES ARTS DE L'ONTARIO

 Canada Council   Conseil des Arts
for the Arts   du Canada

Published by
Second Story Press
720 Bathurst Street, Suite 301
Toronto, Ontario
M5S 2R4
www.secondstorypress.on.ca

Printed in Canada

Contents

Introduction

Carolyn Foster

THE PUBLISHER of this anthology was struck by how many of the stories were about love, and I was struck by the appearance of spaghetti in several of the pieces. And the two, love and spaghetti, seem to be linked. In the "spaghetti stories" there is almost something ritualistic about this link: the boyfriend makes spaghetti for his girlfriend before the relationship breaks up. Hence, the subtitle of the anthology.

This anthology, however, is not really about love and spaghetti. Or, is it?

Essentially, this anthology is about a new generation of women writers in Canada. My aim as editor was to collect an accurate sample of the writing that is being done right now among twenty- and thirty-something women in this country. I was also looking for writing that was imbued with a literary quality. That is, these aren't stories you'd find in *Bridget Jones's Diary*. What I was looking for was good writing. What I wanted to find out was who these women are. What are they writing about? And how are they writing about it?

Of course, all this newness and discovery is in comparison to something else. Something that has come before. The matriarchs of Canadian literature. The writers I grew up reading and, later, as a student, studied and wrote about. We all know the names: Atwood, Munro, Laurence, Shields, also Urquhart, Gowdy and Michaels.

It was more so the first three of these, Atwood, Munro and Laurence, that I feel shaped what Canadian literature is for me. The words of these writers also helped shape my Canadian identity, which is no small feat. The first English essay I ever wrote was on Margaret Laurence. The assignment was well-timed—around the time of her death—and my source material was the myriad of newspaper articles that came out after she died. *A Bird in the House* became my favourite book. And I visited her hometown of Neepawa, Manitoba, and wondered about the life of this smoking, drinking, tough, lonely old broad. Who, for me, wrote magically.

When I was in my mid-twenties, after growing up with these women and this literature, I began to wonder about *my* generation. Who was writing in my generation? I knew the themes and ways of Atwood, Laurence and Munro: the mix of post-colonialist and feminist ideals, the painful ties with one's family of origin, and the task of getting out from behind your husband to do your own thing. But what were the women of my generation writing about? I wondered. Before I could answer that question, there was this question: is there anyone my age writing stories I'd *want* to read?

As part of a creative writing course I was taking at the

University of Toronto, we read stories from the *Journey Prize Anthology*, 1999. The winner that year was Alissa York for *The Back of the Bear's Mouth*. This was the beginning of an answer to my question. After reading that story, which I enjoyed, the proverbial light bulb went on. *So, this is what is happening, and yes, there is something happening.*

Since coming across York's story, and in doing research for this anthology, I have been impressed at the abundance of writing going on in this country by young women. And also that a lot of the writing is good and certainly goes above and beyond the parameters of *chicklit*. (Which when pronounced aloud to myself I think of little tablets of gum that I found to be cute and flavourful as a kid.)

Back to the subtitle. At first I thought the appearance of spaghetti in several of the pieces was simply a quirky coincidence, rather than a minor theme of the anthology. But, as to finding out the answer to my question of what my generation of women writers are writing about (my other question had been answered—they *are* writing), perhaps it is a key.

What has changed since Margaret Laurence sat in her little house in rural Ontario chain-smoking and chugging away at her typewriter? The post-colonial world is now a global community. Globalization, globalization and more globalization seems to be the order of the day. Much of the groundbreaking feminist work that needed to be done feels as if it has been done. The struggle of women to be taken seriously and valued does not feel as exigent in my generation (in my country). And women writers are not setting up house at a young age and then needing to break away in order to exercise their artistic, writerly selves. (Well, some may be, but that situation doesn't seem to pervade the writing.)

I don't want to over-analyze what my generation is about compared to my mother's generation. I don't claim to know this. I couldn't, as a generation is made up of so many different experiences and my world is only a small world among many, many worlds. Also, I don't want to pit the generations against one another; as with differences, there are always similarities. That said, one more note on spaghetti.

We are the pasta generation, not the meat-and-potatoes generation; the generation in which men cook (or are supposed to, or, there certainly isn't any stigma attached to it—there is even motivation to do so to be an independent yet nurturing 21st century kind of guy). And, we are the *disposable* generation, in which relationships begin and end like the blade in your razor starts with a sharpness and ends when it gets dull.

Hence these stories of Thai food, a pickle fork, ground sheets, hockey hair and hymns, rice crackers, a Butoh dancer, old-growth forests, crickets and a Welsh mountain pony, fish pee, answering machines, broccoli florets, an Elvis doll, miniature booze bottles, non-babies, Shirley Temples and mermaids, theses, IKEA, condoms, futons, oxygen, rain, the Aurora Borealis, a ceramic hula girl, angels, olive loaf, ferro cement, tree lines, Georgian Bay, grandmothers, combat boots and tea.

As for who the women are, read the anthology and you'll see.

My Monkey

Annabel Lyon

I CAN LOOK OVER my shoulders at my twenties, bits of
my twenties are still stuck in my teeth, but I know I'm getting
older because here: I'm dating people with children. Can this
be right?

I'm at Patel's with my date and his ex and their kid. My
date has gone to the men's. The kid is telling us there's a new
girl in his class named Hedwig. "Head Wig," he says, making
it into two words so we won't miss it.

"In German, this is a very beautiful name, pronounced
Hed-*veeg*," the ex says. She's blond. So, fine.

"Hedwig, like a wig on a head," the kid says, not malicious
but struck. "What do you think, Claire?" he asks politely.

"Reminds me of lice," I say.

Our server comes and writes down the incomprehensi-
bles we've ordered. "To what level?" she wants to know.

"Hot, hot, hot," the kid says. "Claire, yes?"

I go to the men's and knock on the door. "Barry?" I call. "What level of spice?"

He opens up. This guy—mine now, I suppose, or potentially—has a beard and a tired face. He's drying his hands on some paper towel. "Seven levels of spice."

"I like your kid," I tell him.

"She likes my kid," he tells the toilet.

I know Barry from a couple of parties.

Back at the table the kid is earnestly eating pappadam. His face is pale and he seems to feel the burden of entertaining us lies on his little self. "I have a joke!" he says, chewing chewing chewing.

I wipe some crumbs off my hand.

"I sprayed," he says. "I'm really sorry."

"Kurt," the ex says. The kid smacks his palm on his forehead, a real smack, like he wants to stick something up there. "Kurt!" she says.

"Petra," Barry says.

"No," Petra says. Now they're having an argument.

"What's your joke?" I say.

"What's a clothes-horse?" Kurt says.

"Kurt," Barry and Petra say together.

"Me." Streaked hair, stretchy pants, black puffy coat. Come on, I see myself.

"Tell us about your work," Petra says, leaning on the "your" like we've just finished discussing everybody else's. Barry starts massaging his temples with his long fingers like he's so intelligent it's hurting.

"Well," I say. I'm struggling with my coat, trying to hook it onto the back of my chair as I shrug out of it.

"Is that real Chinese?" Kurt wants to know.

We all look at my little chest. "Well, I think so," I say.

"I like orange and blue," Kurt says. "And pink and green and black."

"And purple," I say. "See? By this dragon guy here, on my sleeve."

"Fangs," Kurt says. "Fangs, fangs, fangs. Arrr." He digs hooked fingers into Barry's arm.

"I think you're drinking my water," Petra says. I offer her mine. "But you drank from that one, too."

I look at Barry for help. "She spat in mine," he says.

Kurt laughs until he snorts. "Kurt," Petra says. He smacks himself on the forehead.

"I'm an actress," I say, a complete lie. Barry looks at me in panic. "However, I balance the flakiness of being an actress by working on a PhD in my spare time." This is true. "Legal ethics, in particular theories of punishment. Retributive justice, aboriginal sentencing circles, shit like that."

"Please don't say that word," Petra says. "Now or in the future."

"Which word?" Kurt says.

"I don't need this," Petra tells Barry. "You know I don't need this."

Why is she here? I'll tell you why she's here. Barry says the divorce was hard on Kurt, that Kurt is quiveringly sensitive to potential sources of conflict between his parents, that I am the first new person to come along for either of them and Petra thinks the kid might adjust better if he doesn't feel meeting new people is some kind of betrayal or covert operation, with somebody getting left out. I told Barry that's what a romance was, people getting left out, but he got stuck on the word "romance," got happy on it, and the conversation degenerated, so I never quite derailed this train before it got into the station. So.

"More naan?" Barry asks. "Claire, yes?"

I take more excellent naan. As in, you've got to go there, the naan is excellent. One wall here is mirror and the ceiling is hung with grubby orange paper lanterns. There are those burlap-and-sequin doings of elephants on the walls and an arrangement by the door with a massive foggy bottle of Black Label for a centrepiece. Personally, as adoptive cultures go, I'm more comfortable with things far Eastern, but then I'm Vancouver-born.

Petra is smoothing her ironed blond hair down around her peanut head with both hands. Up by the ceiling sitar sounds jangle over a wash of electronica. "So, investment counselling," I say to Petra.

"You're interested?"

Someone kicks me under the table, a kneecapper. I do the physics and figure it's Kurt, but his face shows nothing. "Absolutely."

"Well, I don't give free advice."

"Neither do I," Kurt says quickly.

"That's too bad," I tell Kurt. "I was going to ask you all about the dot-com sector and make a killing while denying you a commission. That's the kind of wicked witch I am."

"Barry," Petra says sharply.

"With a name like Hedwig, there must be a tradeoff. I bet she's extremely pretty or cute."

Kurt slides down in his chair, slinky-spined, until all we

can see is the top of his head. Then that disappears too. I push
my own chair back and duck under the table and there he is,
staring right at me with his round, Barry eyes. He says, "Hey."

"Hi."

"She has red hair."

"Wow."

"Don't tell my dad."

Barry's knees are khaki, Petra's bleached denim.

"Do you think we have enough oxygen to stay down
here?"

"Check your tank gauge," I tell him.

He pretends to look at something over his shoulder, then
says, "Almost empty." I think, What a noble, elegant kid.
Above us are hissing and whispering, surf sounds.

"What's your joke?" I ask him, but he disappears back up.
His knees are khaki too, which on a nine-year-old looks like
formal wear.

When I surface I see Petra has secured herself a fresh
glass of water. My own two glasses have been relocated, side
by side above my fork. Barry looks up from his empty plate
and levels a look at me I can only hope Petra sees and Kurt
doesn't because neither of them has a place in it.

"Ah," Petra says, a dry sound, something clicking into
place in the system. She's seen the server coming across the
room with our food. We all sit up a little straighter.

Technically I'm an interdisciplinary student, which means I
shuttle back and forth between departments, donning and
shucking personas on the fly.

My thesis advisor in law is a guy named Slade. He says,

"Have I mentioned how much money you could be making in the real world?"

He says, "What do you think of this tie?"

He says, "Belgium? Who gives a fuck how they do it in Belgium?"

"For comparative purposes," I explain.

"OK, but not Belgium," he says. "America. You want to get hired when you get out of here, don't you? You want to get hired in Belgium?"

Slade's office is a grand illusion. In the School of Law, a grim sixties building of angular textured concrete and coffee-coloured skylights, pocked vinyl and sour shag, he has a Persian rug, pinpoint halogens and teak accoutrements. He can close the door and sit in here and pretend he's still, legally speaking, one expensive whore.

I know he distrusts me because after my law degree I went straight into academia instead of articling. He suggests some recent UK case law I might want to look at. "You're light on case law," he says. "Those pathetic pinkos in ethics are brainwashing you into abandoning appropriate sources. Dworkin, Rawls, who cares? *Stare decisis,* you know that. No case law, no case."

"Yes, sir," I say.

"Belgium is rank cheese and strippers."

"That's Holland, sir," I say.

He's old and not old, silver hair and tan hide. Ambition persists. He tosses my thesis aside and leans forward, eyes burning and watering like a believer. "Miss Fellows, don't you want an expense account and minions?"

"I want time for my personal life, sir."

"Don't be innocent," Slade says.

Outside the air is softly brown and the leaves on the ground look bluish. It's November, it's cold. I stride across campus, seeing the buildings as great stone bubbles of heat.

My thesis advisor in philosophy is a guy named Franco, Franco Ferry, an acknowledged genius who thinks the words "penal policy" are hilarious.

"Oh my God," I say, slumping onto the sofa in his office. "Did he call me a commie bastard again?"

"It's not his fault he's old. How do you know where I was, anyway?" He runs a finger up and down his shirt front, meaning my clothes. Franco himself is wearing rugby pants—rugby pants!—and a white shirt striped with red like a candy cane, the starched short sleeves of which stand out from his skinny shoulders like fledgling wings. I tell him, "Hey, I look good."

There's a knock at the door. "Go away!" Franco yells. "I'm sexually harassing Claire!"

The door opens anyway. It's Denby (metaphysics, Kant, tenure). He looks at me and says, "Professor Slade."

"This is a nice suit!" I protest.

"It's a nice uniform." This from a man in polar fleece. He looks over Franco's shoulder at Slade's red marks all over my thesis.

"What I want to know is, if he hates teaching so much, why does he teach?" Franco says finally. "You know? If he loves practising so much, why doesn't he practise?"

"He got disbarred," I say. "Alcoholic."

"I thought you had to basically kill somebody to get disbarred," Franco says.

"He did. Impaired driving. His fourteen-year-old son."

Franco's face swings to the window, eyes closed, like I've dealt him a blow to the jaw.

"Lost everything," Denby says. He knows the story. "His career, his marriage. Estranged from his family. Excellent mind. Tragic."

I'm watching Franco. There's something of the bad penny about him, something jittery and unstable, for all his laurels, and something funky and rotten, overacted, about his reaction now. I love him, of course, but I keep an eye on him also.

"Still drinks," Denby adds softly.

Franco's eyes pop open in annoyance. "That's no good," he says.

An hour later, as I'm leaving, he asks me how my date went. "Bobby, right?" he says. "Barney?"

Among other things—six languages, a PhD at twenty-two, photographic memory—Franco has total recall. "That would be Barry," I say.

"Barry, right!"

"Cut it out, Franco. *Franco.*"

"I bleed," Franco says, grabbing the patch pocket over his heart.

Did I say a complete lie? Is there such a thing? What I am is a movie extra. I've been in *DaVinci's Inquest, The X Files,* and currently I'm in a major motion picture called *Bomb.*

"Promising title," we extras say. We stick our heads out to see if the rain has stopped. The beach is a bleak textured expanse, the sand tanned by the rain, the ocean looking warmer in the cold. Nearby are movie trucks and trailers, spooled cables and young idle people. "No, no, no, stay in the tent!" the AD yells. She wears a garbage-bag poncho and a Lakers baseball cap and squints at the clipboard she's sheathed in a plastic sandwich bag. "Inside, people!" she yells without looking up.

"I am getting mighty tired of that one," my friend Fiona says.

The difference between Fiona and me is that the day I'm finally teaching Nietzsche to sluggish undergrads she'll be the star in the trailer. Another way of saying this is I was born normal but she has to dull down her prettiness for the job, brown lipsticks and such. She actually does something with makeup to make her eyes look smaller so she won't light up her corner of film too brightly. Fey and *espiègle,* these are the words I would use to describe rusty-haired, rusty-voiced, rosy-lipped, baby-eyed Fiona.

The tent they've got us penned in, twenty or so of us, is like a marquee, with a peaked top and plywood floor, but closed on all sides, canvas walls wicking wet to the touch. In here are grey metal folding chairs and a folding table for the coffee urn, stone cold and empty. Our breaths smoke in the cold. We've been here since dawn. There is talk of insurrection, of making a move on the quilted silver catering van. There is dark illicit talk of soup.

"I agree the term is overused," Fiona is saying. We're talking about whether people who are not Nazis can ethically be referred to as Nazis because of certain key personality traits—meanness, Germanness, oppressive tidiness and hygiene, and a need to impose it on others.

"She implied I was inferior."

"She felt threatened."

"They've been divorced for over a year. Divorced means you're not allowed to feel threatened any more. There's no relationship left to threaten."

"Ha," Fiona says. "Although I didn't actually mean her relationship with Barry. I meant her relationship with her son. And personally I would ask for new water too if some stranger drank my water."

"I guess," I say reluctantly.

"Having said that," she says, and I cheer up quite a bit, "she does sound noxious."

"Finally," I say.

"I was getting there. What about the kid?"

Rain patters harder. "Hopeful. You could tell he just assumed things were going to work out."

"And you don't?"

The AD with the clipboard shoves under the tarp across the doorway. Even drenched, her braids rest hiply on her clavicles. These people. "Gather round!" she's yelling.

"How do you stop an elephant from charging?" I ask Fiona.

We're being sent home. "I actually have no idea," Fiona says. We file out of the circus tent and onto the wet caked sand. The tops of the cedars beyond the parking lot are lost in haze. Not one minute of film did they shoot this day.

"Take away his credit card."

"Do you need a ride?"

"It's a joke."

Fiona drops me half a block from my building, where I can hop out on a red. When the light changes I walk along beside her for some paces. "Don't be depressed, Claire," she calls through the window. Around us the city has that blue kinetic rush and jam of late afternoon traffic. I wave and turn around and there's Barry, sitting on the steps of my building.

"Are you depressed?" he asks.

"OK," I say. "Maybe a little."

"We never debriefed," he says. "After that dinner thing, which I admit was pretty bad."

"Actually, you're right, it was."

I can tell he's surprised at that. He stands up and we face each other, me with my keys in my hand. "Hey," he says.

The party, the party. This was last month. People know people know people and suddenly here's this Barry guy, giving me looks, making conversation. I remember drinking white wine from a fine glass, a glass I had mock-complimented our hostess on earlier in the evening because we were all old enough to be drinking wine instead of beer but young enough that IKEA was still a force in all our lives, old enough to covet luxuries but young enough to savour that slight tart rind of irony we all had a taste for. Then this Barry says something about his sitter and suddenly we're all standing around on a windswept plain in our fancy dress-up clothes, feeling lost.

The next party, this is two weeks later, two weeks ago, and I'm late, oh, miserably late, rushing up the walk from the east whereas this Barry, Barry, is rushing up from the west, and we meet in front of the condo-complex door (this is my friend, the party-giver, who lives in the funky habitat), too cutely. Of course we don't go to the party, either of us, but go drinking together, of course, and get pretty waxed (Barry tells me afterwards he was nervous), so that from there to meeting the kid was the shortest possible distance between two misjudgements.

"Am I coming in?" he wants to know now.

"Barry," I say.

My apartment way up there is pretty good, pretty empty: paper lanterns, the futon, the framed New Yorker covers. Books on ethics, books on punishment. I do have condoms, but that's not the issue, is it?

"Here's the thing," I say.

"Shut up," Barry says.

Denby and I fly to a conference in Guelph. "I think the retributivists should wear red and the utilitarians should wear blue and we should play football about it," Denby says, meaning soccer.

I deliver my paper before lunch and hit the few questions out of the park. I ditch the buffet and take a coffee outside to sit in the minus-five sunshine and read an article I've been saving about Chief Justice McLachlan.

"You terrified those nice old chaps, Claire," Denby says, finding me. He has a large eggish head and a rather fluting Englishness, though years in Canada have made his "r"s nice and firm. "You should be in there angling for a job. Every possible suspect in your field is back in that room. They'd like to come out and talk to you, but they're afraid after you bit that Yank's head off."

"I might actually *be* a lawyer," I tell him. "In the core of my being. I could still article."

"Slade," Denby says.

"I'm still quite young. Many, many doors are open for me right now. Depending on what I do, some of those doors could close. Would that be good?"

He closes his eyes. "I quote: 'If she starts moaning about articling, tell her to call me.'" He opens his eyes and shrugs apologetically.

"Franco should meet Slade," I say. "Franco should meet someone he can't squish. I should arrange something."

The door to the conference hall opens, spilling a passel of philosophers who spot us and wave and wait.

"See what I mean?" Denby says.

"Something innocent, a party," I say.

Fiona arrives first. "Hey, nice," she says. I've swagged silver tinsel over the doorways and left the blinds open for the sight of the Christmas lights beading the buildings opposite. I've put food all over the table and candles in the bathroom.

"People do this kind of stuff sometimes!" I say because she's smiling at me.

Next comes Denby with a large poinsettia. "Ha," he says when I introduce him to Fiona.

Next comes Franco and a girl he calls Tash. Tash wears a gingham duster over her hair. Tash has a pierced eyebrow. Tash possibly has a driver's licence. "Hey, is that Professor Denby?" Tash says. "I am such a fan! I am so going to start a fan club! When he has to answer questions in class? And gets all embarrassed and stutters?"

Franco watches her trip over to where Denby is plucking at the plant. Franco's shirt has little pictures of shirts on it and his tie little pictures of ties.

"Franco." I squint at him. "Is that a student?"

He grins in a way I'm sure he thinks is crookedly. "Just a little one."

"Franco," I say, but the door goes again.

It's Slade, Slade sober, Slade burdened with pink roses to break my heart. "Miss Fellows," he says.

"I didn't think you would come," is what falls out of my mouth.

"This is work. I don't miss work. Where's the red devil?"

I gesture through the roses. "Professor Slade, Professor Ferry."

"Cinnamon bun!" Franco says. He's just spotted Fiona.

I tell him she's just a monkey like the rest of us.

"Franco," Franco says, transferring his attention back to Slade. They shake hands. Other introductions. To Fiona Slade says, "Cute." To Tash he says, "My God, woman, what have you got on your face?" Then he goes for the eggnog.

"Whoa, whoa, whoa," Franco says. "Come right back here, Claire."

The last of my guests arrive: Barry, Petra, Kurt. For them the tinsel, the samosas, the scrubbed tub, the Charlie Brown Christmas music. "Claire!" Kurt says, handing me a box of chocolates. "It's very nice to see you again."

Barry and Kurt are wearing khakis and sweaters. Petra wears a suede dress over a turtleneck, belt, tights and boots, all brown. "So, these are your friends," she says.

Barry follows me into the bedroom so he can give me a hug after I lay the coats on the bed.

We go back out and right away things are good because Petra asks Barry where the bathroom is and he can say, "I've never been here before, you have to ask Claire."

When she's gone Franco comes over and says, "It's Barry!"

"It's Franco!" Barry says right back, rattling him. Poor Franco is not having a good night. Barry kisses my cheek and goes over to talk to Denby and Slade. Tash and Kurt are playing paper scissors rock and in the kitchen I hear what must be Fiona taking something out of the oven. "You never used to let me kiss you in public," Franco is saying.

"I never used to let you kiss me."

"I thought that was the ombudsman."

"Both of us. About Tash over there—"

"They make a nice pair, don't they?" He means her and Kurt playing the finger games.

"I'm glad you see that."

"I see that," Franco says.

An hour later he's back, tugging at my sleeve. "You have to article," he says.

I look over at Slade, but he and Petra are off in a corner, leaning together, talking intensely. "Hey, do you see that?" I say, nudging Barry.

"I've been seeing that," he says.

Franco goes over to stand behind Tash and smooth her hair into a ponytail under the duster, making her look piratical, running his fingers behind her ears, over and over, while she talks to Fiona. After a while she shrugs and waggles her head, wanting him to stop, and he says, "Stand still, woman."

"Your Franco's kind of odd, isn't he," Barry says.

"Franco's never met a smart person who despises academia, like Slade. I think he's having a paradigm shift."

"He does realize he's not supposed to fiddle with his students?"

"He realizes. Who's got Kurt tonight?"

"Petra. Why?"

Then he gets it, and touches my foot with his foot.

"Where is Kurt, anyway?"

Kurt's in the bedroom, sitting on a space he's made by pushing the coats aside. "Hi, Claire," he says. "I hope you don't mind. I was just taking a rest."

"I understand," I tell him.

"Claire," he says, "who's the man in the suit who was sitting with my mom?"

"Mr. Slade?"

"He kissed me," Kurt says.

"Ah, he did?" I say.

"Right on top of my head while he was shaking my hand. My mom laughed."

I sit beside him. It's nice in the dark. I want to lie back on the coats but decide not to because I'll have his daddy in here later. "How's Hedwig?" I say.

"We call her Hedy now."

"Hedy, right," I say, like I'm remembering something obvious. "Do you like her?"

"Yes."

"Do you like me?"

He hesitates. "No."

We sit in the dark and listen to the party sounds through the wall.

"Sorry," he says. He smacks himself on the forehead.

"I find it really annoying when you do that," I tell him, and then we both feel quite a bit better.

Love in Two Pieces

Kristen den Hartog

part one

IN THE MOMENTS before he dies, the sheet comes un-
tucked and out poke his long, bare feet. They hang over the
edge of the hospital bed, pale and heavy, and Irene holds one
in each hand. It's how she knows he is going: his two released
feet and his mouth, gently smiling. His baby toes are tiny for
a big man, with just a sliver of nail. Irene squeezes each foot,
bends and kisses them in turn. This is goodbye, a long time
coming but come too soon. Today they removed the tubes for
his breathing and the one that puts food in his veins, though
it looks like plain water. Steak-man, pie-man, he never would
have eaten that. Now, tubes gone, he resembles himself to give
her one last look. If it weren't for the bland room and the
nurses, Irene could believe he was sleeping, that any moment
he might rise up and hold his arms out for waltzing. And there

she would be, head to his chest, ear finding, hearing, feeling the buzz of his voice box. This is what she thinks of as he leaves her: Bart and Irene waltzing.

Bartholomew Finn was a popular man. Many years ago he owned the hardware store, and though there is a big one now, miles high, people remember him, apron on, in the shop. Neighbours who are strangers come for tea and triangle sandwiches and Irene stands with a china cup in her hand, alarmed by the multitude. Her daughter and her granddaughter are somewhere here, among the million ants who swarm in the open spaces, though this is the private home of Bart and Irene Finn. Like backward ants they bring and do not take away the anemic sandwiches, the crackers and the bright orange cheese which they themselves devour. Like ants each one looks the same as the next, smiling sadly. Someone is in every corner, a neighbourstranger on every chair and three in a row on the little sofa. Irene's cheeks hurt from smiling back at the matching smiles, and behind her mouth and eyes are the hiding words *Go away please go away now please thank you.* Not until they leave can she go to the bedroom and touch the shirts and pants hanging long and tidy in the closet beside her own clothes, but she is thinking of them, the wool tweeds, the patched cardigan elbows, the many empty skins of him. For now there are people lurking in the hallway, on the way from here to there, sighing and shaking their heads. Her own thudding heart scoops words from the swirl of gossip around her, and so she hears only fragments of murmur float by. "Such an odd little ... what will she ... tremendous man ..." She should take part, discuss. *Yes he was a tremendous man you cannot even begin to know how tremendous a man he was so go away now please thank you.* She keeps her mouth closed and her lips smiling so the wrong rude words will stay within her. What the right words are for such an occasion she does not know. Bart would. He could talk to a neighbourstranger or even a total stranger until the cows—that was what he would say. Until the cows come home. But if Bart were here, the ants would not be. Though once there was a writhing mass of them, spilling in from the baseboards and forming a black swell of river on their kitchen floor. She can see Bart bending over them and pouring on the baking powder to smother them in unexpected snow. Turning to rapscallion-grin and when his mouth opens and the words fall out it is just as though he is living. "Ha! That'll show them," he says. She can see his pink tongue talking, his chest rise-falling, and how fine it would be to reach and touch the broad chest and the breath and the heart beating, indisputable signs of life.

"Hello! I said, hi there."

Evan? Ewan? Aside from her daughter and granddaughter, he is the only not-ant here. He has a fresh smile, sorrow-free, and he gives it to her.

"Hello," she says.

"Hi. I just wanted to say I'm—"

"My granddaughter loves you," says Irene.

The man smiles. "I know," he says. "Listen, I just wanted to tell you—"

"Are you Ewan or Evan?" she asks, wrinkling her whole face into a question.

The man smiles the beautiful smile. "Evan," he says.

"Oh. That's too bad. Ewan is nice. Nicer than Evan."

"Oh well," says Evan. "Listen, if you ever—"

"Not me," she says, and holds her hand up in the sign for stop. "I plan to be just fine."

Evan squeezes her hand and then leaves her. She watches him wade through the ants, out the door and across the yard to the garden, where her granddaughter stands. Her kitchen window makes a picture of them. Evan's arms wrap around Reenie, Irene's namesake, and Irene feels Bart's arms enclose her in the safe black wash of embracing.

After the ants go marching, she sits on the sofa and inhales the silence. *What now?* she thinks. And then she says it aloud, testing the sound of her voice in a home without Bart.

"What now?"

In the grocery store, sugar sprays all over, coats the floor like drifted snow. The image of the ants comes back and Bart appears again, *Ha! That'll show them,* mouth moving, heart beating. Irene stands bewildered, holding the empty bag.

"Cleanup on Aisle 4!"

So much noise, lights buzzing, people shouting, cash registers humming. She wants to reach up and cup her ears but is frozen, can't move. A boy who appears too young to work a broom comes to sweep the mess away. Her mess. "I'll do that," she says, reaching to grab, but he grabs back and glares at her. "Crazy," he mutters, and something else she can't hear. Irene wants to say sorry, that the bag must have had a hole in it or been sliced open by some hooligan, but all she recalls is the spray of white, and the hot spread of blood beneath her cheeks and neck. Grief or decay she does not know. Perhaps she is an old sweater or a mitten, eaten by a moth. Moths eating holes in her memory.

"Gimme the bag, lady."

He looks irritated, as if he's had to repeat himself too many times, though she's only heard him this once. *Who is the child,* she thinks, *me or you,* but this she does not say. He tugs the bag from her hand and rolls his eyes. Irene stares at his pimples, an astonishing plethora. So many, so sore. She can't think why she needed sugar anyway. Bart ate a lot of it, in tea, on rhubarb, on noodles with butter. Would wet his finger and dip it into the sugar bowl for a snack between meals. For a long time he went without teeth, lips sunken into his scruffy old-man's head, the head she loved and held in her hands. And then he died. She was holding his feet then, she remembers it well. She kissed them goodbye and then she moved up to his face and kissed his lips goodbye too, knowing he would not have minded, feet, lips, a fine order. "There are no rules for kissing," he said a thousand years ago, "except for one: there are no rules for kissing." And he grabs her around the waist so firmly her ribs might snap, her hat falling off and tumbling to the ground, but as quickly as the image comes, it goes, and Irene wanders to the next aisle.

Salmon. She holds the can, shakes it, water sloshing around inside like in a full belly. *All the things you can think of with salmon in them—go:* salmon mousse, salmon-salad sandwiches, spawning salmons, salmon bones, sockeye salmon, salmon steaks on the barbecue, Bart's big hairy hand squeezing lemon onto them, sizzling and spitting. "The juice of one lemon makes 'em tangy every time." He winks, chefish-ly kisses his fingers. Irene won't eat salmon now. Prefers tuna. Without Bart she's afraid of choking on the bones—no one there to save her. Bart saved her life once when she half-swallowed a whole mushroom cap at a party circa 1952. He was yammering on in that way he had and when he turned to include her in his mirth he saw her wild eyes, her breathless red face. Man of action, up he rose, his chair toppling over be-hind him. He wrapped himself around her and forced the food out with his fist digging into the pit of her stomach. Again the feeling of him crushing her ribs. They made their way like that to the washroom, the two of them joined and moving as one person, shocked guests watching from the table. The cap came out whole, perfect, as it was when sucked in by her laughter. They looked at it floating in the toilet bowl. Bart had teeth then, and a tear in the corner of each puffy brown eye. *Couldn't bear to lose you, Reen. Couldn't stand to be alone.* And then his hands on her, mouth pressing down on mouth, big fingers in her hair holding on for dear life. Long life.

In the produce aisle Irene fingers the squeaky broccoli florets. All the vegetables lie sorted like gems in bins, topaz, rubies, emeralds pulled right out of the flat brown ground. Soggy and faded when you cook them too long, all the life boiled out of them. Bart didn't want false teeth. She cooked everything three times as long as she had before and then put it in the blender, meat too. So sad to see it. Everything a soupy mess. "All goes down the same hole, my sweet." Bart a grown man eating baby food. But that's what life was, a circle, like a year or a waltz, but longer. No surprise when he went because he had been going for years. Bits of him withered and failed altogether but he kept on grinning and winking, always winking. Wrinkled hand on the broccoli, she drifts off and finds herself later among the lemons, looking for him there. Runs her hands over the mounds of yellow. Lemons drop to the floor, bouncing, rolling, bruising.

"Cleanup in produce!"

Irene stands aside as the same boy with no heart scoops up the lemons and mutters who knows what or why. Little Tin Man, he works quickly, too quickly, stomps off. She can see lemons left behind here and there, one beneath her cart, one more over by the oranges, masquerading, and another that's rolled its way down to the vegetable section. *Go, go*, she thinks. She bends her stick legs, snatches a lemon and holds it, cool and weighty in her palm.

A trip to the grocery store—a cab there and back, which is expensive—and all she has is a lemon, which she did not buy but stole. She put it in her pocket and held her hand around it and scooted through the store and out the OUT door and into a taxi. All the way home zooming through the streets and past the living moving laughing people she held the secret lemon, a crime that fit in her pocket. Now she is sitting on the sofa once more. Her feet pressed against the floor and her hands holding the cushion because she feels lightweight, light as air.

Like a dustball she might rise up, float off. Nothing grounding her now with his big shoes empty and all of his soft clothes flat with the loss of him. Summer skins, winter skins. Ninety-eight and Bart was sharp as a tack but without him she is crazy. "You were always crazy," says he from somewhere other than his old blue recliner. He used to cover her up so no one could see, and now without him she is all barenaked. Her clothes have fallen off and the craziness she kept in her sleeves flies like leaves through the neighbourhood. Landing anywhere, seen by anyone. "Not all there," said the neighbourstrangers. "What will she do?"

Halves of a whole where now there is a hole. Only his body gave out, and her body is fine. Little, brittle, it gets her around. She can bend and touch her toes but she can no longer play the piano, not always. The black-dot notes like black dots, nothing more. Tall and strong, Bartholomew fell to pieces. He had big knees and a deep, round belly button that only grew deeper, rounder with age. Irena-Thumbelina curled in there, going with him. Or stretched out along the hollow of his collar bone, hiding in the ridge of his ear.

In the beginning he had been the strapping man and she the wily female. *We will buy this lot on this street and you will build us a garden and a house with rooms large enough for dancing.* Every month she put the hardware numbers in columns in books, adding, subtracting, carrying over. Years and years of that. She could make hardware-number wallpaper with the sheets she filled. Brain, brawn, brawn, brain, they moved into each other and out the other side, and here she is with her muscles that can carry a load and her mind that brings home one lemon for groceries. The sour flesh and the pits. Outside and inside, weeds are taking over. Dandelions growing in her head and her garden. Six feet under, the dangling roots of flowers tickle his wasted body. Waste, what a waste, with his mind still working.

Irene puts the lone lemon in the fruit bowl, chooses a record and leaves the arm up so it plays over and over. And then she steps, turns, sways with the music. One-two-three, one-two-three. *What a dancer you are!* he whispers, brown eyes crinkling at the edges. *Oh go on,* Irene tells him, but what she means is *go on and on.*

Circa 1930 and Irene wins contest after contest with Hank, a boy-man, he has one eye that looks at you, in you, and another that rolls and stares elsewhere. Hank in a plaid suit, whisking her around the dance floor until she is flying, champagne dress whirling around her ankles. Hank's pale face beaming when they know they are winning, even right in the middle of a dance. And then later looming over her, his face a luminous cock-eyed moon, lusty tongue sticking out. *This is not love,* thinks she, but all the time spent in his long skinny arms makes it almost natural. And she is twenty-seven, oozing desire. Long dancer's neck pressed with kisses and a warm Hankish onion smell she does not love but as another kind of partner he is beyond compare, and she has the two confused just now, believing one (dance) cannot exist without the other (romance) because she has not yet seen Bartholomew Finn with his pockety hardware apron and his two left feet in enormous rubber boots. For now, for years, she is in green satin, blue satin, pink satin, gold satin, green shoes, blue shoes, pink shoes, gold shoes, and Hank, grinning, is beside her, each with their ribbons for waltzing. Yesterday, a million worlds ago.

And then grey November and she is in her grey hat and grey coat and grey scarf that turn the grey of her eyes from dull to extraordinary. She is on a trolley, riding by incognito, and Bartholomew Finn, a stranger, is in his best borrowed suit, standing on a street corner. He has been placed there by friends so that Irene can have a look at him, decide from a distance, and though his pants and his sleeves are too short, she seeks him out on a later grey day. She sashays into the hardware store, Finn's, and says anonymously, "I need to buy a key, please," and she finds that he might as well be nine feet tall, a friendly giant before his time, and beautiful in that far-from-beautiful way that proves the heart has eyes. Here before her are his elephant ears, his crooked gargantuan nose. She brings the key back four times to exchange it for a different one. "I'm not sure why," she says, "but they just don't seem to be working." Which of course is impossible, they are skeleton keys, they open everything. But each time the giant exchanges the key willingly, wishing it too will be returned. By the fourth time he feels brash and flirty enough to say, "Maybe this fella's not worthy of a key," and Irene's face is a hot strawberry smiling.

Then began a long ordinary life of loving in which Irene grew iridescent eyes.

One-two-three, one-two-three. She is teaching Bartholomew to waltz. His two left feet are more stubborn than clumsy, and he does not believe there should be rules for dancing. He is wearing his soft corduroy pants, the brown ones which he will own forever. "One-two-three what?" he says. "One-two-three where?" and lifts her up and flops her over his shoulder like a spinning laughing sack of potatoes.

Night and the memory moth is searching for Irene Finn. Frantic flutter to the light but Irene is in the darkest corner, not ready to be eaten. Last year, when it grew cold she pulled Bart's mittens from the storage box but when he put them on and held them up the left one was full of holes. He said, "It's full of holes," and turned it to show her. Then he laughed and turned it back towards himself and said, "How can something be *full* of *holes*?" They had been his very favourites, warm, with mismatching stripes. She might have known then that he'd be going. But how is it that he can be gone when she can see him in his polar bear parka and his big hands with the uneaten mittens are rounding the snow into snowballs for throwing, even though a little part of her asks is it not summer, the season of his demise? Here he is, though, packing the snow into a smooth ball and the fat red stripes on the blue mittens are fatter on the right than on the soon-to-be-eaten left, it's why he chose them, and the ball is spinning through the frostbite air and passing another, just kissing it, which means that she is there too, a snowball playmate, rather than here in his blue recliner, where every night she sleeps alone. She closes her eyes and reclines. All that remains are the mixed-up mind's home movies and this chair, smelling of him, and the faceless

Bartholomew ghosts that are his pants and sweaters.

"Yoo-hoo," says she. "Yoo-hoo!"

Hot summer day circa now and she is in the garden, looking for him once more, Bartholomew Finn among the weeds
and the sunflowers, which is over-the-top foolish, even she
knows it, but just the same, there he is. You never know, do
you? Lovers meet, meet again in the strangest places. He is
standing with the tallest sunflowers in the garden, and jester
that he is he moves his head in that sunflower motion, east to
west. How crazy. In his rubber boots with his pant legs cloud-
ing out the top like a Cossack, he holds his arms out for waltzing, and out loud she says, "No, no, with you in those pants we
should dance that Russian kicking dance, shall we?" But as
she moves toward him and reaches to touch the old smiling
cheek with the palm of her hand, the rough brown nubbles of
the sunflower centre ooze from his mouth and cover his lips
like blisters, and then his eyes and all of his missing face and
now he has yellow petals for hair.

And of course she is weeping.

A man she has seen in a picture comes out of the picture
and across the yard toward her, carrying an armload of
flowers.

"You look like a bride," she says, wiping her nose with
her sleeve.

Evan smiles the beautiful smile. "Are you okay?" he asks.
A funny question because she is sitting red-eyed in the weed-
filled garden with yellow petals in her white snow hair.

"Yes," she says. "Thank you."

"These are for you," he says. "Reenie asked me to bring them from our garden."

"Oh."

"She had to work late but she'll be here soon. Should we put them in water meanwhile?"

"Yes," she says, "we should."

And then there are flowers sprouting out of her kitchen table and her little bedside table.

"You must miss him very much," says Evan, having sat with her at the table for two.

"Yes," she says, sipping. "I do."

In the lucid aftermath she is in bed, wearing Bart's pyjamas with the legs that go on forever, and smelling the wide-open apricot roses that sit in a jar on her bedside table. Evan and Reenie opened the windows before they went home, so the air is once more in motion. If Bart is in the dust motes he is flying now, up and out the open window, briefly back in with the late-summer breeze but then out again, and away. She is not hurting, yet she is not soaring either. She can no longer imagine Bart's living face, how it looked in the garden before the blisters made him any old sunflower. She cannot see him throwing snowballs or murdering ants, but she knows he was elated in those visionary gifts. Gifts that might fall again from nowhere. In the moving pictures he is more than alive, though even then he is dying. All our lives we are dying. Out falls our hair like the turning leaves, but for us there is no spring coming. No better reason for living it up. *We lived it up, eh Reen?* said he without teeth. The sores on his atrophied hands like stigmata, *first sores I ever got from doin' nothin'*, but yes we lived, she told him, we lived it up. Now she can find only his dying face. Bartholomew Finn, husband in a soft blue gown, white hospital sheet spread brightly over him. Long, now, instead of tall, because like a baby he was always lying down. By way of goodbye she traced his sinking face with her finger, over the forehead and nose, the laugh-kissing lips, the bristly chin and the old loose neck. The head-rest chest, the concave belly and the hip bones jutting. Long pencil legs and the big bare feet, two lefts, where the boots used to be. Such a massive erosion. Three goodbye kisses, foot, foot, face, and that was that, that was all. She came home without him. And now, without him, on she goes.

part two

WHAT HAPPENED when Evan left was that Reenie began hearing voices. Just low murmurs, louder near the door of her apartment than anywhere else, which made her think they must be coming from outside. Every hour or so, that first night she heard them, she tiptoed over to the peephole and looked into the hallway, but no one was there. The voices were accompanied by sweet, strange music, barely audible, the echo settling in Reenie's mind. The last thing she wanted now was music, but it kept floating toward her. Unhappier than she had ever been, she was always humming. She knew the lyrics of songs she had never heard before, old songs like *By the liiiiight of the silvery mooooon, I want to spoooon with my honey and crooon love's tune.* That was what she wanted, to spoon with him. Everything here still smelled of him, it might always.

The leaving had been quick, as though arranged ahead of time. Reenie arrived home from work and saw that Evan had made spaghetti. There were tulips on the table, gaping in the steamy kitchen heat. It was spring. Flowers were coming up everywhere. He set the plates down, sat in his usual place across from her, ate in his usual way, chewing slowly.

And then he said: "I've met someone."

If she could rewind to that point, she would. People met people all the time. It could mean anything. She could say, "Oh yeah? Who?" and he could say, "His name is Dave. We're going to play squash together every Monday." And the rhythm would continue, except that Mondays he would be with Dave and Reenie would be calmly reading, not crying, not breathing his smell on the sheets, though washed and bleached. Not sensing his presence, and so his absence, in every unseen molecule in the air.

Instead he said: "I'm leaving."

Now there was no one who knew her. Evan left and he took nearly everything he'd come with. Little gaps appeared in their shared closet, in her heart, on their shelves full of books. All of his books had his initials inside them, E.M. When had he done that? And why? She wondered if now she might not have babies, if her one aborted try had been her only chance, if her womb and her breasts had been wasted, and what kind of woman she was for thinking such a thing.

Everyone smiled and said "Plenty of fish—" but she held up her hand to stop them. She hated the thought that people were replaceable, like light bulbs.

Spring kept coming. Flowers pushed through the soil, and in her own garden there was Tulipa Princess Irene, first the thick new leaves and then the bloom, orange bleeding into purple. She had planted them for their name, which was hers and her grandmother's (not princess, but Irene). Irene had gone into a home last year, just as the tulips faded. Irene was fading too, fading fast.

Days Reenie worked and evenings she turned invisible. She walked unnoticed through the streets until her legs ached. Starved, she wanted to eat the spring, the songs of birds, the moving river. Maybe she was from the river, and had washed up on shore with a see-through shell around her see-through self. If she reached to touch something, she would touch the wall of the shell. If she spoke, people wouldn't hear her. Perhaps just her mouth would appear, and they would see it moving like Clara Bow's, the silenced heart-shaped lips. And yet, she could hear them. They rushed by her, laughing with their mouths stretched open. They sat at patios with the new spring sun shining down on them. They touched hands and tasted each other's food. Reenie was afraid of seeing Evan here, with her, whoever she was. Someone. When she thought about that for long enough, the fear sent her back inside, though it hurt to be still. Walking made it seem as though life continued to happen without him. When she stopped, when she came back home and put her key in the door and stepped into the room that still smelled of him, of herself, of herself and him together, the whole world slowed and warped. And always there was that muffled music—violins and warbly voices. She plugged her ears to see if she could still hear it, and, no, she couldn't, so she wasn't crazy, it was coming from somewhere, but she searched pointlessly and then she sat on the floor and cried.

Once she had read that the brain worked like a seesaw. When you got wild with sorrow or rage, the blood rushed away from the sensible part that made you reason and concentrate, and it pooled in your emotional part. Stagnant stinking pool of sadness. But that was all she could remember. Surely if the term "seesaw" had been used, it meant the blood would spill back again and she would be, if not happy, at least rational and unsad. She thought, not laughing, your heart is all through you, even in your brain, you can't get away from it. When you get a cut, your heart is right there, pulsing in the opened flesh. It's everywhere. That must be what skin is for, to keep your heart contained. And when she thought about her heart and how big it was, how much it had loved him, she would suddenly find she had called him at work to tell him just that. Clutching the receiver. Sitting on the floor as she told him, looking at her toes and the chipped polish.

"Remember the day we won Elvis at the CNE?" she asked, sobbing. "How we belted him in in the back seat and all the way home he looked out the side window, remember?" Like a baby, she thought, but she did not say. Laughing, crying, she continued. "We kept asking him how he liked the scenery. And we sang all those songs, like a *hunka-hunka*—"

"Yeah," said Evan, laughing softly. "I remember. Of course I remember."

Afterwards she couldn't believe she had called. She held the buzzing receiver in her hand and stared at the little black holes in the mouthpiece. She opened the closet and looked up at Elvis's plastic face on the shelf. His black plastic eyes with the crescents of blue.

As quickly, she could balloon with anger. Call him and say, *"Just don't ever call me again. Don't ever try to see me, not ever."*

And there would only be his breathing, his waiting.

"I mean it," Reenie screamed.

All he did was sigh. "Reen, I'm at work," he said in a too-gentle voice. "I can't talk about this now."

And Reenie sobbed and sobbed. "When can you?" she said softly. Spluttered "Please, when can you?"

In a seesaw haze, she missed him and loathed him. She stayed up late, drinking from their old collection of miniature booze bottles and singing all the Elvis songs she knew, which were many, more than she had ever imagined. By the end of the night she could twitch her lip. She wished she could show him that. He would laugh and shake his head in that way he did, which said she was crazy and that he adored her, who could not? But she could not imagine kissing his mouth, now that his tongue had been in Someone's mouth, and she could not imagine lying on top of him, not anymore and not ever again.

 ℰ

Reenie had been left with the cat, Juniper, who had been his before they met, but although Juniper had known him, she had not ever loved him. Once, without reason, Juniper had lashed out at him, and her claw had sliced open some important vein in his nose. The blood had shot straight out, in pumping jets, which was his heart beating. It was hard to believe, now, that he had a heart, and was a living, breathing human. That he breathed into Someone's mouth when he kissed her.

A daydream: Juniper opened Evan's jugular with her claw, and Evan died from the gaping wound. Last year, before Someone. Reenie grieved, much the way she was grieving now, but with dignity and reason.

Reenie's grandmother Irene believed a body got only so many breaths in life, but that you never knew the number until you'd breathed your last one. Once you'd used them all up, that was that. No more air, no more living. Which was why it was important to breathe slowly. "Bartholomew breathed too quickly," she had said when her husband died. "I told him and told him, but he kept right on." Reenie had held Irene's hand at the funeral, smiling inwardly, since her grandfather had lived to ninety-nine. Now she thought about all the times she herself had hyperventilated, about all the extra air she had taken in only to let it out too quickly. Her time was diminishing, and she had used up three years of breath on Evan, believing he'd meant every lovely thing he'd told her.

ℰ

"Marry me," he said.

"Okay," she said.

He didn't ask, which made him seem not arrogant but all the more sure of what he wanted. He was lying beside her in a tent on Flowerpot Island. He looked right into her and grinned. The sun shone through the nylon and turned their bodies blue. Outside lapped the waters of Georgian Bay. Reenie folded her fingers with his. She didn't doubt that they would be together always. If she could, she would rewind to the blue world of that moment.

ℰ

She had planned to wear Irene's wedding dress, long, bias-cut, plain except for the poofy sleeves. But he had laughed when she modelled it and said she looked like she had cream puffs growing out of her shoulders. He didn't seem to know she'd been serious.

"You look like you're trying to be Greta Garbo," he said.

Those were the key words: trying to be. Without them, the sentence would have been totally different. Reenie was constantly surprised by how completely you could change a thing by lifting part of it out. Still, she laughed. She hunched one poofy shoulder and peered at him sultrily. She mimicked Greta Garbo as best she could, swooning with her hand on her forehead.

"I vant to be alone," she told him, sweeping from the room in her too-big dress.

And he called out behind her, "That was Dietrich!" Laughing so hard he snorted.

For a long time Reenie stood in the other room, staring at herself. Only after he'd moved out did she realize that she, not he, had been right: Greta Garbo, Grand Hotel, 193?. She considered calling Evan to gloat, but the thought of Someone answering the phone stopped her.

Reenie and Evan never got around to getting married, but once when they were drinking wine and playing Scrabble she saw his young face turn into his old-man's face, yet to be. He was choosing letters for a word and she was watching him grow wrinkles and longer ears.

"Do you know how I know we'll always be together?" she asked him.

"Do tell," he said, smirking.

"I can see you when you're old. I know just how you'll look, exactly."

It didn't matter that they hadn't married, not until after he'd gone, when she wondered, did it make you try harder, being husband and wife? She had loved him. She had felt she was a physical part of him, and he of her, which perhaps was wrong and more than anyone wanted. But since his departure, their time together had begun to warp into make-believe, as though all along they were only playing house, and then the game was done, and they could go and play with someone else. With Someone. Now is an erosive era. People bought plastic disposable razors and drank their coffee on the move out of doubled paper cups because a single cup was too hot to hold and they had to go, they couldn't stay, they were all in a hurry. Everything was take-out, pick-up, drive-through. Empty plastic bags flew like birds when it was windy, and wound up hanging from trees. Her grandparents had been married sixty-nine years, and would have kept on being married forever if one had not died. Reenie guessed they were still married, depending on how you looked at it. But Irene was in a home now, she had vacant rheumy eyes.

"There he goes," she'd said as they'd lowered Bartholomew into the ground. She'd linked her skinny arm with Reenie's arm and leaned toward the hole. "Bye my chum."

And that night in bed Reenie had said to Evan, "You're my best friend, you know." Her lips touched his ear because though he was sleeping, he might feel the shape of her words.

Tulip petals dry in the form of a heart when you press them. Reenie knows because her grandmother did that. She has her grandmother's scrapbook. It and the dress were given to her when Irene moved into the nursing home, where there was no room for keepsakes. In the book there are beautiful cards from the thirties, some with ribbons attached. The drawings are plain and elegant, like the drawings on old sewing patterns. It seems impossible that a card made now could ever hold the same beauty years into the future. But maybe these also seemed like silly old Hallmarks then. Bart had signed every card "?", from 1930 right up until 2000, when he died. Sometimes you had to look to find the "?". It might be on the hidden inside, on the back, under the flap of the envelope, even penned on a ribbon. Reenie had looked through the scrapbook as a child, but she hadn't known about the "?" until the book had become hers. She sat with it on her lap, discovering card after card and smiling. She was so enchanted she felt her heart expand.

Bart was found for Irene by friends who insisted he was dreamy and divine. They were each in their late twenties, an unusual age to be single in those days. Bartholomew owned a hardware store, and Irene was a shopclerk/dancer. She was so reluctant to meet him that her friends arranged a drive-by viewing. Bart stood on the corner in short brown pants and an ill-fitting charcoal jacket, and Irene rode slowly by on the trolley. She could see that he was looking for her, scanning every face in the hope of knowing who she was before he knew her.

"He looked ridiculous," said Irene to Reenie. "His suit was awful but he had a rose in his lapel. He kept leaning his head towards it and sniff-sniffing, but still looking all around for me. I knew when I saw him sniffing and looking that he had to be Mr. Right."

Reenie no longer knew about right, about wrong. Before he left, when it still seemed impossible that he would go at all,

Reenie said to Evan, "I don't understand how this can be happening. It just seems so right with us. Doesn't it? I mean, hasn't it always felt right?"

Evan sighed. He touched her hair, which made him seem kind. "I want something that's more than right, Reenie. I think we owe that to ourselves, don't you?"

She said nothing, because how could she? What was more than right? Less than right was wrong, she knew that, but what was more?

Yes, Reenie was constantly surprised by how completely you could change a thing by lifting part of it out. She feigned astonishment when he told her, "I'm leaving," but months before she had dreamed of flying away. They were living in an open-concept sphere and they could not stop smiling. Because the floors were curved, getting around was difficult. Reenie had to walk very carefully so as not to tip the sphere. Evan was less careful. With his frozen smile he looked down on two cockroaches mating. Whenever their bodies touched, the brown bugs turned iridescent silver and blue. "Look at that," he said to Reenie through his smiling clenched teeth. And then he put out his foot and slammed it down on them, because after all, they were pests. A rancid smell arose. The upset sphere rolled and rolled. All of their books fell from the shelves and dishes rained from the cupboards. Reenie closed her eyes and tumbled. When the sphere stopped rolling she looked for him. He was sitting with his back to her, rubbing his head. She pushed open a window and flew out and didn't look down again until the sphere was a dot, and then nothing.

When she woke up, she felt sick and guilty. She let the dream flutter off and smiled.

"Good morning," she said, and then kissed him.

The post-Evan dreams were also strange, stranger than normal. Sometimes they were exactly true. More than once she woke up, sweating out a memory.

"I'm pregnant," she told him. Her smile here was wide and genuine, unreturned. This in their second happy year.

Not ready, no, not that I don't love you, some day we will, not now.

Pain in his face and voice, and so in Reenie's.

And Reenie sees herself at the clinic alone with her hat and coat on because it is the colourless middle of winter. He isn't here, not in the dream and not in the memory, but only because she asked him not to come. In the sweaty, wake-up, after-dream time, she thinks he should have come anyway. He should have been there. Of course she believes in choice. Deeply buried, almost disposed of, is the knowledge that she made his choice rather than her own.

She has always been annoyingly dreamy. People have said, and she knows it herself. She can remember thinking, as a teenage girl, that one day she would own a love that was unreal, fabulous, not realizing, of course, that unreal was not real, imaginary, illusive; and that fabulous was incredible, exagger-ated, absurd. Every morning Evan blew his nose in the shower and the first time she heard it—*"Hawwwnk!"*—she was ap-palled. She sat still in bed, blinking, her face contorted in a horrified grimace. She wanted to believe that theirs was a love that was out of this world. They were mad for each other, crazy in love, Catherine and Heathcliff. And yet the real story was printed on the page in lucid black and white: Catherine loved Heathcliff but he was rude and dirty, so she married her pale, effeminate neighbour instead. Heathcliff, enraged, ran off with the man's sister, whose puppy he'd strung from a tree. Soon Catherine died in childbirth. Heathcliff loved her so completely that later he dug her up. "I'll have her in my arms again! If she be cold, I'll think it is this north wind that chills me; and if she be motionless, it is sleep." Who wanted that? Perhaps only sane, ordinary love was everlasting, thus extraor-dinary.

Reenie's own parents had divorced when she was eleven. Her father wept and hung his head and claimed to be sick of love, but soon enough he was hungry again. Her mother swore off men. "Men are for the birds," she said, and Reenie wondered (*still* wondered) how birds came to be connected with things we don't want or need. Birds ate crumbs, but they also flew. They sang in trilling coloratura and many mated for life.

❧

Reenie was waiting now, humming to the everpresent music. Letting time go by because everyone said that was all it took.

She thought of how, in stories, the girl always pulled herself together and the guy came snivelling back, begging to love her again, only to see with dismay that she was effervescent, thriving without him, and, most devastating of all, happy to have run into him and wondering what was new. When she was still with Evan, Reenie wondered why the make-believe girl could never get happy without the make-believe guy wanting her back. "It's insulting," she'd said to Evan. "Same theme, over and over." But here she was. Humming and daydreaming. Dreaming herself cheerful and Evan so maudlin that the blood pumped through him slowly, almost pointlessly, now that his heart had lost her. His heart a deflating balloon.

She stopped humming but the song played on. Was it inside or outside her head? She followed the swelling muted music. It took her over to the door again, made her look through the peephole. She saw nothing but the bare hall and a muddy pair of gardening boots, but she could still hear the music. She opened the door and poked her head out. The music was definitely inside the apartment. Now her heart was beating fast, she could feel it in her fingers. The phone rang and she jumped back. She let it ring until the answering machine clicked on, but instead of hearing her own voice, "Hi, this is Reenie," the music grew louder. She leaned closer to the machine. She could barely hear herself below the warbling music, and then she heard Evan, watered down by violins: "... me ... if you're ... how you're ... don't ... cheer you ... Bye."

Reenie stood with her mouth open. The red light flashed. Evan hung up and the music faded again. She touched the volume dial, thinking she could hear the song louder, but turning it simply changed stations.

℮

"Anyway, it turned out to be my answering machine," she told her grandmother. "Crossed wires or something. It's really old, so no wonder. Most people don't even have answering machines anymore. Well they do, but they're invisible, you just press the numbers on your phone to—"

"Huh?"

Reenie looked at Irene's raised eyebrows, white and full of questions.

"My answering machine," she said again. "It was playing the radio."

"Oh, yes," said Irene. "I see."

Reenie was sitting with Irene in the nursing home. She leaned forward and slipped her hand into Irene's, which was growing soft and babyish and seemed almost void of bones and muscle. Irene looked at her blankly. She slid her hand out from Reenie's and used her fingers to spread her other hand open. She showed Reenie her white palm and said, "This is the first sore I ever got from doing nothing," though there was no sore there.

Reenie smiled. She wanted to cry, but didn't. Irene was fading away. Reenie had often seen her sit and look at her trembling hands, turning them over in her lap as though they could not possibly belong to her, to Irene the dancer.

She didn't tell Irene much about Evan, except to say that things had not worked out. "People don't stay together forever anymore. I think it's because of cell phones and drive-throughs and debit cards and disposable contact lenses and maybe even the inter—"

"You know, we had an answering machine," said Irene.

"What?" said Reenie.

"We had one. I didn't like it at all. All that beep-beep and the stop and start. After he died I shut it off, who needs it?" She waved her hand to show her easy dismissal of the thing. "I went the whole rest of the year without that thing turned on!" The grey of her eyes deepened. "And then one day I decided to move the blue lamp next to the phone, since I was always talking to you in the dark, you see, and so I got it over and I dangled the cord down behind the table and then I went around the other side and crouched down to plug it in, but what I plugged in was that silly machine. All the click-click-whir started up and the light was flashing so I started pressing buttons to make it stop, and who do I hear but my Barto. *Honey it's me,* he said. *I'll be home soon.* Irene paused and looked at Reenie. "For a second I really thought he was coming."

Toward the end of the visit, when the conversation had turned to rain and Reenie's mother and red hair and televisions, Irene said, "I never liked him anyway."

"Who?"

"You know," said Irene. She flapped her bony hands, trying to recall. "Ewan."

"Evan?"

"Evan, Ewan." Again she waved her hand in that dismissive way.

"Why?"

Irene shrugged. "He had a big head."

"What do you mean? You mean he was full of himself?"

"No," said Irene. "I mean he had a big head."

Driving home, she cried laughing. Every make-believe thing was in pieces now, like a puzzle, but somehow less puzzling. Each specific piece with its shape and meaning. The non-wedding for which only she had dressed up. The non-baby, removed and discarded. She turned the radio loud. She thought about Irene, disappearing, yes, but perhaps a princess after all. And she thought about the music breaking through on her own answering machine. Music always broke through, she should have known that. Evan wasn't here now, and the baby in the back seat had been painted and made from plastic. Reenie sang. On she went without them.

Bottle Episode

Dana Bath

I KISS JOE'S SLEEPING face and he murmurs, "You have to tell her today, babe."

I slip out of the hotel to take the SkyTrain to Waterfront Station, where my mother and my mother's girlfriend are waiting for me in front of a yellow half-school bus. As soon as I see them I have a seizure of regret, thinking of Joe still asleep, long and heavy and warm in the crumpled sheets, while I'm out here with all the anger and cold and damp in the world. The sky hangs close and grey. Pat and Addie, outfitted in warm green and black, are stiff little chess-piece figures against the yellow side of the bus.

As we stand waiting for someone to tell us what to do, I light a cigarette. Pat says nothing, which is admirable. A ragged man leaning against the building near us is watching me, and I give him a nod. He puts his fingers to his lips and pulls them away again in a smoking gesture. I hold the pack out toward him; he trots to me and takes two.

"What's your name, honey?" he asks.

"Lisa. And yours?"

He shakes his head. "Got a light?"

I've put my lighter back in my bag and can't seem to find it. The man holds out his hand for my cigarette and I give it to him. He lights his own from it, hands it back to me, bows his head in thanks and shuffles away down the street. I'm about to put the cigarette back to my lips, but Pat plucks it from my fingers and tosses it to the ground.

"Do you know," she said, "that forty-six per cent of people don't wash their hands after going to the bathroom?"

"Where the hell did that number come from?" I mumble, but her expression of horror is so sincere that I let it go and don't light another.

Last time I came to Vancouver to visit Pat, I took an afternoon to walk alone down to Granville and Howe to meet a friend. I turned onto Pender from Main and a man came out of an alley and followed me. It was the middle of the day, but I looked over my shoulder anyhow and he said, "Don't be afraid of me, dear, I'm not going to hurt you." He had beautiful straight coffee-brown hair almost down to his waist, no shirt or shoes, eyes like black pinwheels. He walked me fourteen blocks and told me about dealing junk, about his ex-wife and his children he hadn't seen for twelve years. He told me about his client the social worker, who shot up in the company bathroom between appointments. "I told him," he said, "that he's living a lie, saying to people they have to give it up when he's fucked up himself all the time. Excuse the language, miss. A lie like that will eat up your soul. You have to be true; you have to have principles. I don't deal to kids, and I don't deal to anyone who deals to kids. I give money to people who have less than me." He stopped, bent down, plucked something from the sidewalk, put it in his pocket. "I don't expect anything from anyone that I don't expect from myself." When we got to Granville, I said, "Well, I have to turn here," and he said, "It was very nice talking to you, miss," and when I looked back he was waiting for the light to change, standing straight, his long hair ruffling.

When I got back to Pat's place that evening and told the story, Pat said, "I wonder why he chose you."

Pat and Addie take a seat together; I take the empty one behind them. A tall white bony man with a shaved white head stumbles on with a fat pack like a pillow on his back. He pulls the pack off and falls into the seat next to me, stuffing the bag down like a cork between his knees. "Greetings, friend," he says. "My name is Warren. Pleased to meet you." He lays his head against the back of the seat, closes his eyes and falls asleep.

I watch Vancouver turn into trees, big shadowy prickly trees, starting sparse but then thickening by the thousands, climbing up the rockside hills and drooping under the weight of the damp sky. The guides stand up and introduce themselves, explain a little about the surrounding landscape: Douglas fir, lava canyons, waterfalls, the Coast Mountains and the Howe Sound fjord. I watch the trees.

When I was a baby and colicky at night, Pat would put me

in the car and drive me around until I fell asleep. It never took more than a few minutes.

Addie turns around to offer me a piece of fruit log. She is barely older than me and looks a bit like me. People sometimes point this out before realizing how inappropriate it is to say such a thing. A lock of Addie's short blond hair is sticking out on one side and there's a smudge down the middle of one lens of her glasses. I try to break off a piece of the log, but it's rubbery and sprays coconut, and in twisting my morsel free I manage to fire it into the face of one of the passengers across the aisle. Warren, next to me, wakes up with a start, his bald head jerking forward. Addie is nonplussed for a moment, and then holds out the fruit log to him. "Much obliged," says Warren, breaking off a generous piece and popping it into his mouth. "And who are you ladies and where are you from?"

Addie and I introduce ourselves. Pat doesn't turn around. "Enchantay, enchantay," says Warren, chewing his fruit log and spraying spit a little. "I am from Spokane myself, but have been living in Japan for many years now." He pauses. Addie and I nod. "I am a Butoh dancer," he pronounces. He pauses again.

"I see," I say.

"Do you know what a Butoh dancer is?" A scrap of pink fruit log is clinging to his lip.

"Yes," says Addie.

"Ah. Well, good for you. And what do you do?"

The back of my neck grows cold and hot.

"I'm a caterer," Addie says. "And I import European antiques and refinish them and sell them to the wealthy at exorbitant prices."

I stare at her. When Warren looks away to wipe his mouth with the back of his big bony hand, Addie winks at me. Pat turns to look at Addie with sudden interest.

I grin and say, "I'm in medical school, but what I really want is to be a scuba-diving instructor. I'm thinking of making a career change before it's too late."

Pat's eyes, large and jealous hazel, peer at me over the back of the seat. She looks at Addie, and then back at me again. "Children," she says. "Stop your silly games."

We pause in Squamish for a pee break. In the gas station toilet, I vomit three times, thinly and biliously. I watch my face in the dark, smudged mirror as I wipe my mouth, then watch my mouth forming one set of words and then another. The rims of my eyes are so dark and painful that I don't see why my mouth has to say anything.

I call Joe. When he answers the phone, his mouth is full and he swallows. "What's up?" he shouts. "Is everything okay? Has your mother convinced you to leave me?"

"My mother isn't talking much. I can't tell if it's because I've pissed her off or because she feels guilty about not inviting you."

"Does she not want to meet me or do you not want her to meet me?"

I look out at the parking lot, where Pat and Addie are huddled over cups of coffee. Warren is standing with them, gesticulating toward the sky, the filling station, the pavement. Addie nods and asks him a question, her blonde eyebrows drawing together under her glasses. Pat's face is a blank.

When I told Pat about Joe, over dinner at a Japanese restaurant when I arrived last week, I told her that he was abrasive, and loud, and large. "On the surface," I said. I cursed myself for making excuses, but it's important to prepare Pat for things. "You can't imagine, Mom, how he loves me," I said.

"And how do you love him?" Pat asked.

"As I've never loved anyone before."

"Hmmm." Pat peered into the dish of sashimi as though she might be able to read someone's future there. "But that's how we always love, isn't it." And we didn't discuss it further.

"Hello?" Joe barks.

"I don't know. I'm afraid you'll hate each other."

"How could she hate me? I'm so utterly charming."

"You'll be with her for five minutes before you're yelling good-naturedly about white-haired dykes and the lesbian separatist agenda, making jokes about how terrified she is of you, and she'll turn into a hissing harpy. I have to get back to the bus. I'm sitting next to a Butoh dancer from Spokane named Warren."

Joe bursts into a guffaw. "That is priceless. What the hell's a Butoh dancer?"

In the bus Addie and Pat break out the rice crackers and Warren is delighted that we have not only heard of rice crackers but eat them. He pulls a packet of photos out of his overstuffed backpack and hands them to me one by one, explaining their history and gesturing that I should pass them to the rest of the bus, who look bemused and uncertain as the photos begin drifting their way. Looking around, I think of something Joe once told me about the "bottle episode," an installment in a TV series when a number of people are caught together someplace, and no one new can enter, and no one there can leave.

"Here I am performing in Fukui. I forget the name of the theatre. And this is in Edinburgh, at the dance festival ... oh, here's one, this is my favorite, it's in the Koraku-en garden in Okayama. I designed all the costumes myself ..." His bald head is almost touching my shoulder as he leans too far to point to the images I can already see. Several of the photos are blurred. Addie has turned mostly around in her seat and takes the pictures from me, nodding, and at Warren's gesticulatory insistence passes them to the people in the seat in front of us. Pat would no doubt be staring out the window, but Addie is by the window, so Pat has to make do with staring straight ahead.

"I'll show you when we get there," he says. "Have you ever seen Butoh?"

"Yes," I say.

"Well, you'll see. I've brought some costumes with me." He pats his fat pillow backpack, but then he stops short. He leans forward and peers into my eyes. "You have very beautiful blue eyes, my dear. In Japan you'd be a star with eyes like that, although many people would be afraid of you."

"Thank you," I say. Pat glances over her shoulder with a smirk, but Addie tilts her cropped blonde head to one side and looks from me to Warren thoughtfully. Warren smiles, his white face serene. I wonder if maybe he took some calming medication earlier and it's only just kicked in. Then I notice that his eyebrows have been shaved off.

"They are not happy eyes," he says. "In my experience, people with blue eyes so large and brilliant tend to have difficult secrets. And ... ," he looks down at the photos still in my hands and reaches to take them away from me, "... they tend to be extremely nearsighted. In different ways."

The old-growth forest in the Elaho, one of the guides explains as we stand on the logging road about to enter the Douglas Fir Loop, is part of a proposed national park that borders on Whistler and includes the Upper Elaho Valley, which is the largest ancient temperate forest left in the region. The tract includes cedars and Douglas fir that are in some cases more than a thousand years old. Logging companies have already encroached upon the area and tours like this are meant to stimulate awareness. If after this tour you feel concerned about the future of this unique and irreplaceable forest, we will give you some contact addresses ...

I stare up at the sky, which seems low and weighty enough to touch the tops of the enormous trees. I'm shivering. Pat pulls a green Gore-tex jacket out of her backpack and hands it to me. I'm annoyed by this, but I put the jacket on.

We head into the forest, one behind the other like a caravan. I move into the crowd at the head, knowing that Pat and Addie will stay behind to take their time. Warren is a couple of people behind me and I can hear him announcing, "My goodness, I have never seen anything like this. Can you imagine, some of these trees have been here since ... well, since before most anything that we know about! It simply boggles the brain. Lisa! Lisa, sweetheart, come back and look at this wonderful mushroom!"

I look behind me. I step off the path to let a couple of people pass, but it seems that everyone wants to look at the mushroom. It's as large as a honeydew melon, moist and fire-orange, almost pulsing. It looks like a sea creature. "Oh my Lord, the beauties of the world are just endless!" declares Warren, his nose so close to the mushroom that it looks like he might kiss it. The others try to move on, but I stay with Warren until he's ready to leave the mushroom behind. He fondles it a little with the very tips of his fingers, strokes it like a cat, coos. When he finally straightens up, he doesn't seem to notice that he's blocked up half the party, and he doesn't apologize.

He walks behind me and for a while neither of us speak. Then he says, "I hope I didn't offend you, my dear, with that comment about the eyes. It's none of my business, of course, but I have a kind of gift, you see. I tend to know what people are like."

I laugh. "Really." I look over my shoulder at him. He's not laughing. His face is very smooth and white and serious. The lack of eyebrows gives him the look of an extraterrestrial creature surprised by the human condition. He has deep lines around the eyes and mouth; he might not be much older than forty, but he might be sixty. He also has blue eyes, a pale grey-blue brought out by a grey-and-blue bandanna he's tied around his bald head.

"You're a hard one, truth be told," he says. "Why don't you tell me a secret and I'll take it from there. Tell me what you want out of this life."

The person ahead of me hoists himself over a fallen tree. I pull myself up to sit on it and pause a moment, my legs dangling. I pluck at the bark of the tree, watch it leave bits of dead brown tree-skin in splinters on me. Warren waits, as does everyone behind him.

"I'm in love," I say. I give a little self-deprecating laugh. "I don't think I've ever really been in love before."

I pull myself over the log and continue along the path. It takes him a few seconds to catch up. There isn't really room for two abreast, but he tries to pull up alongside me, bumping me presumptuously in the process. "And how do you know you are this time?"

I shrug. I think I feel a spot of rain, but maybe it's the slight wind shaking moisture from the trees. The man ahead of me releases a cedar branch and it wallops me gently in the face. "I care about him more than I do about myself," I say. I push the branch forward and hold it until I feel Warren grasp it.

"That's the first answer I'd expect. What does it mean?" Warren is panting with the effort to stay beside me. The air feels thick and wet, cool yet heavy. I shake myself a little. I almost say, Look, this isn't really what's on my mind. But I can't quite bring myself.

"If he left me, for his own happiness ..." or safety, I think, "... I'd understand. I'd wish him well." I frown at my feet.

"Ah. But that hasn't happened." I shake my head. "And do you expect it will?"

Someone left me once. At first he didn't physically leave— he was still there in the house, rustling the newspaper and sweeping the kitchen and shutting me out of the study, but it was as clear as if he'd stuck a sign on his chest saying, "Back in 5 minutes or when you've gone away, whichever comes later." He used to complain that driving with me was boring as hell because I wouldn't talk; the best I could do was sing along with the radio, and it just wasn't social. I often wonder if he left me because I was no good at small talk. Not long after I'd decided to marry him, he dropped by Pat's house to pick something up or drop something off and Pat didn't invite him in. I wouldn't have known this—he never mentioned it—except that Pat brought it up the next time we talked. I didn't express any interest in the incident, but Pat explained nevertheless, "I don't feel I have to have a relationship with him just because of you. If we're going to connect, it has to be as two individuals. And I don't see that happening."

"Does he plan to marry you?" Warren asks. I stare at him. He grins. His teeth are crooked, and quite yellow. "Your love."

"If he does, he hasn't mentioned it." I sound more affronted than I intended to.

"I'd have him marry you, dear." He nods sagely, his blue eyes steadily on mine until he trips slightly on a tree root and falls a step behind.

I laugh. "I tried marriage. It's not much of a guarantee."

"No, it's not a guarantee." His voice is muffled, and I turn to find him struggling out of a cedar bush that has engulfed him. "Not a guarantee. It's a declaration, that's all."

I hold out a hand and he hoists himself free. "Have you married anyone, Warren?"

"No." He brushes himself, but he's still looking at me as if nothing, not even death or serious injury by cedar, is more important than this conversation. I look ahead again and

continue on my way, and he plods after me. "Not in the traditional sense." I hear him stop behind me and he lays a hand
on my shoulder. "Lisa, dear, look at that."

Ahead of us on the path is a fallen tree. Its trunk is as big
around as ten people lying together in a pile; it's stripped of
bark, polished and grey as the sky. Warren pushes past me
and goes to lay his hands on it.

"This is it," he says. He drops his bulging backpack to the
needles on the ground and shouts, "Everyone! Everyone,
please gather round. I need your attention for a moment."

Warren leaps onto the log and throws his arms to the sky.
"Friends, I would like to perform for you a dance in the Butoh
tradition, in celebration of the marvellous corner of the earth
that we have been given the privilege ..."

At my shoulder, Addie murmurs, "I wasn't aware that
Butoh was a tradition. Wasn't it invented about twenty years
ago?" I smile.

Warren jumps from the log, limbs splayed, and lands on
the path catlike. "Ow," I hear; he holds up one hand, inspects
the palm, plucks at it with a couple of fingers and then opens
his backpack and with several grand flourishes pulls out a
river of lime-green chiffon. He gathers it up in his arms and
gestures with a hand flapping at the wrist for me to come
closer. He passes me the cloud of green fluff and it swallows
me to the top of my head; I try to press it into a more manageable wad as he leaps onto the log again, kicks off his hiking
shoes, pulls off his socks and the bandanna from his bald pate

and drops the whole load on top of me. He crouches and murmurs to me intently, "If you can find the end of the fabric—ah yes, there—please hand it to me and hold on just loosely ..." He pulls out a length, then begins to wrap himself, over shoulder and around waist and then the same again, turning like a gyroscope until he resembles a tall barrel-bellied elf with a stream of green hanging from either shoulder. The breeze picks up the chiffon and moves it behind him like lazy sails.

I look up. The sky, if possible, has moved closer, although maybe it's just the effect of the dark magnitude of trees. Then I feel a speck of rain, for sure this time.

Warren is being the wind. He skitters from one end of the log to the other, his arms outstretched like airplane wings, his chiffon billowing. He's making wind noises between his teeth. He extends one foot ahead of him and hops, on the other, the length of the log, until he slips and lands hard on his backside, which inspires him to stretch his white face silently in a skull-like approximation of Munch's *The Scream*. His chiffon has tangled around one leg, so he takes an elaborate several minutes to untangle it, loop by green loop, still seated with his legs on either side of the enormous tree, and with each movement he spreads his whole body in paroxysms of welcoming joy. Then he stands and begins to creep the length of the log, stopping after each inch to balance and twist on one leg or the other and raise his face to the crowd or to the sky, lips contorting, eyes alternately stretched and shut.

Addie whispers, "I think we are seeing a rather personal conception of the Butoh tradition." I almost burst into laughter.

Pat is standing near us. Her arms are folded and she is smiling slightly with tight lips, her eyes on Warren. I watch her for a moment. Pat's face, under the white bristle of her hair, is long and almost grey in the cold mist of the rain. She looks small, but sturdy, like one of the young cedar bushes dwarfed by the age-old trees.

"Mom," I say.

Pat turns her long grey-brown face my way and my stomach knots. She's tired, I think. She's tired of bad news. Oh my Lord, the bad news of the world is just endless. What if I live a long and happy life? What if there is never any reason for either of us to be afraid?

The night I was attacked on my way back from the university, but managed to get away unscathed, I tumbled home, without crying and without collapsing, to that man who left me, and he sat with me until very late. He made me tea and we watched the television and finally, at about one in the morning, I said, "I want to call my mother."

"Why?" he asked.

I didn't answer. I tried to imagine what sort of answer he wanted.

"You're fine," he said. "There's no need to make her worry." He got up and emptied the teapot. I waited until he went to bed, and then I called Pat.

He left me not long after that. Most of the time, when I think of him, I think of that moment, and wonder if there was something to what he was saying.

I'm crying, I find. I sink onto a stump, and the few people standing near me are spreading away from me like steam fleeing a drop of hot oil. I can still hear Warren's chiffon rustling. I feel Pat's small body close beside me and her arm around my shoulders. I heave, and vomit between my feet onto the forest carpet.

I was ashamed of tears as a child, but when I grew up, at the end of each bad love affair, I found myself running back to Pat's house and staying there for days, lying under a duvet on the sofa and weeping and being comforted with back rubs and rum toddies. I often slept in Pat's bed with her and sometimes we talked late into the night, sometimes cuddled like puppies. Thinking of it now makes my skin creep on my bones. In Pat's murmurs, "I told you so" was buried so deep that only I could ever have discerned it.

I wipe my face and look up. Pat is waiting; beyond her, Warren is throwing his arms and face up to the rain. Pat's eyes are not blue like mine; they're a dark hazel, but they're the same large round shape, although Pat's vision was perfect until several years ago, when her doctor told her she needed bifocals and she laughed at him.

"There's something I need to tell you," I say.

The rain comes down like the sea. Warren, his costume sticking like lime juice, takes a bow.

Congratulations, Really

Heather Birrell

THE RAID IS Katie's idea. Afterwards, and in years to come, she will try to convince herself that it was Tatyana who had somehow wiled her into it without saying a word. Katie knows that this would not have been beyond Tatyana's abilities, but she also knows it is only a slim slice of a larger, more ragged truth.

"We'll put some masks on, and just, I dunno, do some tattoos on their faces. Or toothpaste. Toothpaste might be good." Katie rifles through her makeup bag.

"We should just spy on the counsellors." Tatyana is reclining on Katie's bunk, painting her nails. "I think it's raining."

It is raining; a soft, barely there rain that *shushes* against the roof of the cabin.

"It's just drizzle. C'mon, it's Saturday night." Katie pulls the leg of some long johns she has scissored into a disguise over her head and swings the door wide to show the way. The prospect of being out in the wild of the nighttime woods has opened another secret door inside of her; she is impatient, and eager to impress Tatyana with her boldness.

At the fork of the trail, Tatyana stops and points to the crook of a pine tree. "Shhh, porcupine." They pause for a moment to observe the bristling dark form. "They're really shy."

It is not difficult to get into the boys' cabin; no one locks their doors at camp, and the counsellors have left to smoke cigarettes and play cards in the lodge. Still, the girls take their time, placing more secret-agent-type emphasis on their actions than is perhaps necessary. Once inside, however, they are unnerved by the normalcy of the scene. The cabin is set up exactly like their own, the bunk beds leaning against the walls, towels and sweatshirts dangling from the rafters. There are no tiny tools of beauty scattered here—eyelash curlers, lipsticks, mascara wands—but the same all-purpose flashlights and compasses line the windowsills. The smell is different, though—it is the smell of clean boys' sweat, beery, without the edge of alcohol. But it is not until they look closely at the sleeping shapes on the beds that something snags inside of them. It is a snag and then a surge. A surge of what? Power, yes, at looking down on these small-seeming boys, taken from their taunts and tumbles, laid low by sleep. But, also: a muffled astonishment at the unchecked rustlings and cuddlings of creatures far from their mothers.

"You start at that end, we'll meet in the middle." Tatyana uncaps a black magic marker and walks towards the bunk closest to the door.

Their efforts are unexceptional at first—double lines on the cheeks to denote Indian war paint, a mound of toothpaste

next to the pillow—but, with a few tries, and the boys' continued lack of awareness, they sabotage less gingerly.

"Check this out," Katie hisses. She has ringed her target's
mattress with toothpaste and squiggled sperm-like mounds on
his chin and forehead.

"Almost done," says Tatyana. "You take the last one."

There is something different about the last one. At first,
Katie thinks he must be awake, and is snared for a second in
his accusatory stare. But then she realizes that although his
eyes are open, he is not *seeing* her. He's dead. She feels a not
unpleasant roiling in the space just below her ribcage. His
eyes are so round and bright, afloat in his dark face like twin
suns misplaced in the night. She crouches down next to him
and lays her hand on his forehead. *What does he see?*

"Tatyana," Katie says.

Tatyana does not turn to look until the boy sits up, sleeping bag bunched, the sudden stink of urine wafting from his
lap, his eyes still fixed on some inflexible future.

There will be other points in Katie's life where her hand
will rise, unbidden, to her mouth, as if to contain what? A
shriek? A sharp refusal? A sigh? A wholly inappropriate guffaw? No matter. Hand to mouth, automatic and universal.
This is the first.

Katie's mother and father were not Christians; they were
atheists.

"It means we believe Jesus was a really good man, but he
wasn't the son of anybody who lived in the sky and made

commandments," said her mother. Katie's parents also used to be hippies.

"Jesus was sort of like the original hippie, wandering around in homemade hemp clothes with no real job." There was something slightly unkind in Katie's father's voice, but she could tell he approved of this Jesus lifestyle.

"Not completely a hippie, more of an *activist*," said her mother, and put her arm around her father. "A bit like us in our day, right Jube?"

Jube, short for Jujube, they had told her when she was three. Short for chewy, colours-like-crayons, stick-in-your-molars, sweet-so-sweet sweets. Then, when she was seven, and more likely to understand the implications: "Not really short for Jujube, honey, short for Jew-Boy. We're not Jewish, but your father would sometimes get discriminated against because of his looks."

Jews were not Christians, but they were not atheists, although they also believed Jesus was just some guy. At seven, fully armed with implications, Katie had understood Jesus to be a tall man; he had a long dark curly beard with mashed up jujubes stuck in it. He looked a little like her father, except he spoke more quietly, and his words had a certain sheen to them that made people listen. And now, at thirteen, Katie is being sent to a Baptist church camp.

"Yep, we were activists in our day, alright," said Katie's father.

They weren't very active now, though. Her mother worked three afternoons a week as a naturopath's assistant, and her father had recently retired, a condition Katie found unbearable. He bought a telescope and hung a map of the stars where the wall calendar used to be.

"Check this out, Kate," he'd say, his eyeball fixed to the tiny end of the black tube. "Far out."

Her parents were old. They skittered around the house like dustbunnies. Mostly they left her alone, which was a good thing. Most of the time it was a good thing.

"They're a bunch of Bible thumpers, though, Rick. Lots of conversions and carrying on. And she'll be on an island in Georgian Bay, for Chrissakes." Katie's mother was lying on the floor in corpse position.

"Can't do her much harm. She's her own person. Besides, it's cheap and outdoors. She'll manage." Katie's father looked up briefly from his telescope.

Katie stood in the doorway, wondering about conversions and how the fuck she would manage. So that was it then. There were some things they were not going to tell her. They were just going to allow her to coast out into the world like that. Unprepared. She cleared her throat.

"It says on the list the sleeping bag should be tightly wound in a ground sheet. That it should be waterproof."

"Oh, *man,* they're exaggerating. Just stick it in this." Her father left his constellations for long enough to pass her a Loblaws bag with a torn handle.

She had spent the next three evenings kneeling in her room, a piece of plastic she found in the toolshed spread underneath her like an ice rink, lengths of rope and bungee cord hooked and dangling from her fingers. The sleeping bag was old and army green, with a flannel camouflage-patterned lining. When she tried to roll it the stuffing gathered in stubborn pockets. There were lumps that would not flatten; it took her three nights to force the thing into a more manageable shape. When it was finally finished, she placed the shining, self-contained parcel next to her dresser. It made the top of her skull jive with satisfaction when she woke up every morning and saw it waiting there.

The boat that is to take them over to the island is not a boat, it is a barge. Which means that it is used, mostly, for carrying cargo; a cargo of Christian campers in this case. A thin man with a large head is standing in the barge, waiting for the kids to hand him the suitcases they have lugged over from the underbelly of the bus. The barge is a rusty red colour, and looks, to Katie's citified eye, like the enlarged bottom of a milk carton, perfect for sailing on the rushing gutter waters of a spring thaw. She has her doubts about its reliability in the choppy expanse of bay adjoining the dock. But she follows the others, stepping down into the box, surrendering her bags to the skinny-big-head man. There is a narrow bench around the periphery; Katie finds a spot and leans against her sleeping bag, which she has decided to keep on her person for safe-keeping throughout the journey. A girl she recognizes from the bus sits down beside her and gestures towards the driver.

"That's Chris. Bit slow on the uptake sometimes, y'know? I mean you can pretty much see the hamster running. Hockey hair too. Bad scene."

Hockey hair? Katie's own hamster is sprinting to catch up. But she does not want to fall behind—not now, when it seems there might be some crucial information in the offing. She had kept to herself on the bus to the marina, made sleepy and antisocial by the warmth and the uncomfortable fit of the situation. But now it is beginning to seem necessary, if she is to survive, to seek out clues, perhaps even an ally.

Chris wedges the last of the luggage into the space beneath the bow, and starts the motor without a word to the human cargo. He is smiling though. A good or bad sign? Katie cannot tell.

"This is your first year, right?"

Katie nods to the girl. The barge is now *ka-chugging* out into the waves, and she realizes she is disappointed by the lack of danger in its ponderous momentum.

"Good job with the ground sheet. Last year they, like, threw them overboard to test them." The girl pokes at Katie's sleeping bag. "Where are you from?"

"Toronto." They threw the sleeping bags overboard? Katie feels a momentary rush of vindication.

"I *know,* but what *part?*" The girl has raised her voice.

In exasperation? To compete with the wind? Either way, Katie does not want to risk losing her, this noticer of sleeping bags. "Downtown, pretty much."

"Lucky. I'm from Scarborough. *Scarberia.* My name's Tatyana. It's Russian. You can call me Tat, but not Tit or Tattie. I hate Tattie."

"I'm Katie. How much longer?" The barge rises in slow motion on the swell of a larger vessel, then plonks down again on the other side. The islands look like fancy lady hats that have been tossed from the sky, the windswept pines sprouting like feathers from their edges.

"Ten minutes maybe. Then when we get in we'll have a welcome singalong and get cabin assignments. The singing's pretty good. I think Andy who teaches canoeing is coming back this year. Hottie. You should be aware of the snakes though, the massasaugas. Poisonous rattlesnakes. I saw a huge one outside of A&C." She looks meaningfully at Katie. "That's Arts & Crafts."

"Oh." Katie gives an iffy laugh. She is trying to take cues, but Tatyana is so obliviously professional and offhand.

"I'm not joking. And they're endangered. So basically their lives are worth more than ours. If you see one—they look a little like fox snakes, and they do actually rattle—you have to report it immediately. Then the Parks people come and T&T them. Trap and Tag."

Katie is somewhat resistant to this synopsis of camp life. She changes the subject. "I like your nose ring." A small silver stud glints above Tatyana's left nostril.

"I like your barrette." Tatyana reaches out and presses a finger to Katie's butterfly bobby pin, then leans in toward her. "The other day I was on the bus and this guy sits down next to me, a pretty old guy, and he's being all creepy, checking me out, then he starts yelling at me. *Yelling.*"

Katie realizes Tatyana is waiting for something. Tatyana is waiting for her! "No way."

"Totally. He goes, *Congratulations, you slut! You are trapped. You are trapped in your world of demons and body mutilations. Congratulations!* Right in my face."

"What did you do?"

"I had my compass in my pencil case, so I stabbed him with it just before I got off. Hard, in the leg." Tatyana's voice is trembling.

Don't cry, thinks Katie, please *don't cry.*

"Like, he might have been bleeding. But I didn't check." Tatyana pokes at Katie's sleeping bag for the second time. But she does not look at Katie. Not for what seems like a long while.

Tatyana is waiting for me. "Well," Katie says, "congratulations."

"Yeah." Tatyana raises her head and smiles. "Congratulations." And she gives the sleeping bag a little pat.

Tatyana and Katie stand, their backs to the cabin's large black window, on tiptoe, their torsos twisted so that they can see what is reflected there.

"My butt is so balloony in these pants."

"Just wear a long shirt." Katie is happy with the way her own butt looks, the cheeks nesting snugly behind each of the large back pockets of her jeans. She tugs at her belt loops, inclines her head to the side. This is the only way for them to get the full picture, perched outside on the rock that slopes steeply behind them to the water. The alternative is a makeup mirror clutched at arms' length, made to travel slowly down from head to hips.

Still, the window does not have the sharp-edged clarity of the real thing, and the shapes and shadows inside the cabin make an accurate image reading impossible.

"Is that a smudge, or do I have something weird under my eye?" Tatyana turns to Katie, who examines thoroughly.

"Smudge."

They balance there, silently critiquing, for another few minutes, the rock bearing them impassively up, the sleek waters of the bay lip-lapping below.

"You know what I like about Andy, and maybe it's because he's older and everything, but he's really got a sense of *humour*, you know? I mean his jokes are so not-stupid."

Katie does know what Tatyana means: the way Andy's jokes are continuous and ironic, with none of the question-answer silliness she still, despite herself, finds funny and true. When Andy was joking he said, *There is something particular I know about this world and the people in it.* He spoke in peaks and valleys of wit, somehow absorbed the punchlines into his patter. It was grown-up, the way he joked, which made it seem ever-present and unattainable, like trying to take a snapshot of the atmosphere.

"Are you going to Bible Study?" Tatyana swats at a mosquito feeding on her forearm, then flicks the splayed body from her blood-stained skin.

The chapel is outdoors, on the tip of the island; two rows of logs for pews and a stone pulpit built so that the preacher stands against the backdrop of God's large unbroken sky. Katie and Tatyana sit on the second log from the back and nudge the wood chips into tiny piles with their feet.

> *Love the Lord your God with all your heart*
> *And all your soul, and all your mind, a-a-a-and*
> *Love all mankind …*

There is always the singing.

"All mankind?" Tatyana whispers.

"All mankind." Katie places her hand on Tatyana's knee in affirmation.

"What kind of man?"

"*All* kinds of *man*."

"Congratulations."

And they are off. To contain it, this blissful bubble that begins behind the breastbone, is inconceivable. But they are in chapel. Katie tightens her hold on Tatyana's knee, and Tatyana grabs hold of Katie's wrist. They squeeze each other and look straight into the face of the counsellor, who is quite pretty really, and has just finished reading from the scripture, something about doling out bread or throwing stones.

I will not look at Tatyana. Katie is seized with the desire to do just that. *Now. No.*

On the log in front of her, she sees a heedful black head bobbing and knows it is Theo. Theo is one of the Ugandans, who are at the camp for free because they are refugees. His posture embarrasses her. And the way he is now quoting the Bible back, his English clipped, his white teeth so square and articulate.

"I think he's a believer," says Tatyana.

"Mmm, hmm." Katie still cannot look at her. Theo turns his head, blinks at them, his concentration fractured.

"Bi-zarre." Tatyana sighs, overcome with responsibility or fatigue.

Katie also feels responsible; she wants to take Theo aside, teach him some sense of things here—what falls within the flimsy boundaries of the acceptable. Instead, she considers the counsellor, her well-scrubbed sturdy certainty. And she thinks she wouldn't mind looking like that; sure of her place in the world. Still, she suspects Christianity would make her sluggish. The only other real Christian she knew was a babysitter she had for a few months while her mother was away in

Australia on a walkabout. ("It means just what it says—we'll be walking about, absorbing the culture, the ways of life. Exploration, Kate, it's so essential.")

Katie loved the babysitter. Jan was strangely thin and wore clanky, sharp-edged jewellery, but made up for it by buying Katie miniature tea sets from the Chinese store up the street. At bedtime, she would read from a waxy blue book she pulled from her suede purse—Jesus stories, illustrated in brilliant comic book hues. Sometimes the colours had been stamped slightly askew, so that the people appeared, literally, beside themselves. The lambs always seemed okay though.

"You don't hate anybody, not really," Jan said. "You may dislike them strongly, but you don't hate them. Not truly." From this Katie understood that for Christians, feelings could be modulated and masked, turned up and down by the way you chose to name them.

Once, Katie had watched Jan help an old lady, a stranger, across the street. The lady was walking the way Katie did sometimes to drag out the minutes on the way home from school, placing her feet like decals on the street, edge to careful edge. "Hurry up," Katie had called, safe on the sidewalk, but Jan did not even look up. You had to be slow and helpful, always, if you wanted to feel Jesus' thick good blood moving inside of you.

Kuh-klang. Kuh-klang. Kuh-klang, kuh-klang.

In the morning the bell wakes them. It is *actually* a bell. An oversized bell that hangs from a rod attached to two A-frame supports, with a green-shingled roof over top. A house for the bell. Someone must pull the rope that is attached to the hinge at the top of the bell in order for it to ring. If they pull too hard the bell will swing up and over, changing the steady clanging rhythm into something wild and offbeat. For some indisputable reason the unchecked up-and-over is frowned upon, considered bell-shenanigans. For some other indisputable reason it is considered an honour to be chosen to ring the bell. Katie does not question these reasons, but she refuses to subscribe to the mores and mystique of the bell. In fact, Katie hates the bell.

"I strongly dislike the bell," she says to Tatyana's hammocked form, which sags down above her, the foam of the thin mattress bulging through the rusted wires of the frame.

"Your conditioner or mine?" comes the reply from the bulge, all business. For someone with inclinations towards the slack, Tatyana is remarkably chipper in the morning. Katie can almost hear the *ping* her eyes make as they spring open.

"Yours." Katie sighs, resigned. "It smells like green lifesavers." She pushes her sleeping bag down slightly, tests the air with her shoulder. She can hear the rafter above creaking, and knows Tatyana is preparing for a swinging descent. She closes her eyes and catches the edge of a dream. *A squirrel that is a kidney that is a soccer ball. Scrambling up a tree. Her father caught, hooked on a branch by his belt loop, arm pointing upward, out toward the cosmos.*

"Up, up, and away!" Tatyana pulls the sleeping bag from Katie's body and dangles her bathing suit in her sleep-silted face. "Suit up, baby!"

There are no showers at camp. Instead, there is morning dip. Which sounds like a popsicle, which is a good way to describe the way you feel during and after the thing itself. The girls stumble down the path, juggling unwieldy shampoo bottles and pink plastic soap dishes, hips enveloped in towels whose corners have been neatly tucked into the tight elastic at the waist of their bathing suits. The morning is not yet grown into itself; the air is cold and still holds the wearied swank of night. In the cove, the water is relatively calm, but further out, near Turtle Island, the waves are frothy, slightly malignant.

There is no escaping it; they slide in on the slick rock, hand-over-hand-over-hand along the dock, grasping for the next wooden board, the ice of Georgian Bay inching up their thighs, until, shoulders hunched high, they duck, squealing, under. And when they come up there is still the lathering and scrubbing to be done with: step one, step two, with rinses in between, the soap lending a shimmering patina to the surface around them.

By the time the boys emerge from the trailhead, their hair pointing every which way like the rays of a grade-one sun, the girls are back on shore, dripping, towels turbaned around their heads, or clutched tightly around their shoulders.

"Do not even go near that thing," Tatyana counsels, as they pass the back of the lodge on their way to breakfast. She is referring to one of the only functioning machines at the camp: an ancient laundry wringer that leans up against the porch behind the kitchen. "One guy once lost a whole hand."

Katie can believe it; the wringer is the colour of an iceberg, and as bulky—it has the form and feel of disaster about it.

"But if you ever do get caught in it, there's a reverse button. You'd have to be pretty cool to find it though, while your arm was being mashed. Do you see Andy up there?"

Katie has always known that there are dangers and there
are antidotes, but knowing the antidotes doesn't ever seem to
do anybody much good, really. You just had to hope and, if you
were inclined, pray, that you could be cool, together, that you
were, in some obscure way *prepared*. She's not sure it is particularly helpful to dwell on the dangers—the snakes and the
laundry wringers—for too long.

At breakfast, Katie and Tatyana are separated.

"What a total gyp," says Tatyana, "I'll meet you on the
steps afterwards."

Katie is seated at a table with Theo and a gaggle of girls
from the youngest cabin. They are talking about snakes. Katie
digs into her porridge, which was never something she
thought she would like—it's a dirty white colour, homely and
old-fashioned! But she does like it, hot, with brown sugar, and
just a splash of watery instant milk. And it's the kind of food
you can feel settle inside of you. It comforts her.

"In Africa, the snakes are as big as my leg." Theo seems
to be addressing Katie.

One of the good/bad things about camp is that Katie can
never tell when someone is having her on. It's best, when this
happens, to feign interest in more practical matters. She digs
deeper into her porridge, presses her spoon against a hard
node of brown sugar.

"As big as my leg," he repeats. He is definitely addressing Katie.

"Hmm," she says, chewing energetically.

"Yes, you can run over a snake in your car, *ba-boom, ba-
boom*, and the snake will still live." He pauses.

Theo is waiting for me. "Well ..." Katie says.

"Yes, and if you look back, you will see the snake slide away into the jungle."

"Slither, you mean."

"Hmm?"

"Slither. Snakes don't slide, they slither."

"No, the snake was sliding away." He demonstrates on the table, sliding his arm along in an S-formation, his hand the pretend-head.

"Never mind." Katie searches for and finds Tatyana, who is about to take a bite of toast, holding her mouth wide, teeth bared, so that her lipstick will not blur. Katie tries to catch her eye, but there is too much commotion, what with the cutlery and the scraping of chairs. Soon they will sing the camp hymn and get on with their day.

"I hope you have a good morning, Katie," says Theo.

"You have a good morning too, Theo," Katie replies, surprising herself with her own formality.

"Yes."

"KYBO," Tatyana had instructed, on the way over on the barge, "stands for Keep-Your-Bowels-Open. There's a lot of stupid-ass codes and routines at this camp, but once you learn them you're basically set. There's no privacy in the kybo, so just be prepared to share your bodily functions."

At first Katie couldn't stand it, the tacky violation of sitting side by side, your shorts pooled over your running shoes, the long pause before the piss hit—*plaap-plaap*—the reeking piles at the bottom, the boys (the boys!) eliminating frankly on the other side of the thin plywood separator. But now she doesn't mind so much, especially when Tatyana looks over at her and says, "I gotta take a dump," and they set off together, purposefully, down the trail. Today Henry, a nine-year-old loser from Quebec, follows them.

There are three seats in the KYBO. Tatyana is partial to the middle one because, she says, she feels less trapped. Katie chooses the one farthest from the wide-swinging door, where it is least likely she will be seen with the changing of the guard. They settle and wait. Henry begins to sing.

> *Yankee doodle went to town*
> *Riding on a lady*
> *Pulled her tits*
> *And made her shit*
> *And then she had a baby*

"Too much orange drink at lunch," says Katie.

> *When I die, bury me*
> *Hang my balls on a cherry tree*
> *If they crack, tabernac*
> *Send them back to Radio Shack*

"I lived in Montreal once," says Tatyana and shifts on the seat.

"Parlay-voo?" says Katie. "Shut-da-door."

"It's *'Je t'adore,'*" and I'd appreciate you not being so immature."

"Why'd you live in Montreal?"

"Oh, my mother. There was this guy who said he'd take us to the Caribbean on his sailboat, so we sold everything. I was going to take, like, correspondence courses. But he never showed. Well, he did, but he loaned the sailboat to some idiot Newfie. We stayed at his apartment for a while. He had these totally disgusting curtains. They were puke colour."

"Oh."

Henry has another verse.

> *Old MacDonald sitting on a bench*
> *Picking his balls with a monkey wrench*
> *Wrench got hot, burned his balls*
> *Peed all over his overalls*

Tatyana rolls her eyes. "Loser!" she calls down through the space between her legs.

Henry makes farting noises.

Now Katie rolls her eyes at Tatyana, who shakes her head, then asks, "How does a Newfie hitchhike in the rain?"

"How?"

Tatyana holds out her thumb and, with her other hand, makes a little shelter over top. "Get it?"

"Oh, yeah," says Katie, and reaches for the toilet paper, which unrolls with a soft conk against the wall at each rotation. But she doesn't really get it at all. She looks down at her feet, where two daddy longlegs are performing a gangly pas de deux. Near the door, more tiny red spiders are scattered like an outbreak of measles on the dun-coloured floor. The island is full of them: spiders and snakes. She grabs for her shorts and stands up quickly, zipping the fly. There are times when the things Tatyana says beg questions, or a gesture meaning comfort, but something always stops Katie. A compact private pride, or a realization that evaporates when she tries to name it.

Tatyana pushes the door open. Henry is standing at the

fork in the path, doing a dance, half Indian chief, half chicken. Katie gives him the finger.

"I forgot my bug spray in the cabin, you coming?" Tatyana is asking. As if she needs to.

On the way down to the archery range, Katie begins to sing.

> *We've got Christian lives to live*
> *We've got Jesus' love to give*
> *We've got nothing to hide*
> *Because in him we abide*
>
> *Love!*

"In Him we *abide*?" Tatyana stops, frowns, starts up again, trips over a root.

Katie rights her, brushes a pine needle off her knee. "In Him we live is what it means."

"In Him we live?"

"Yeah, Jesus is like a big container for us all, so we don't have to worry about anything."

"Congratulations, you are trapped," says Tatyana.

They hold their breaths as they pass the KYBO.

"Allow me to congratulate you," Katie says, on the other side.

They link arms.

To get to the archery range you must cross over the blueberry flats, where the scrubby low bushes with their tiny round fruits offer some respite from the bare bulgy rock and hot sun. The trail markers are old but effective, their concrete bases and hot pink tips plainly pointing the way. Once past the flats, the terrain becomes marshy and treed; planks bridge the more moist parts of the path. The archery range is set up in a clearing next to a small bog, the targets nailed firmly to a row of spindly pines. The shade, the mulch, the mould and humidity—all are ideal for the rapid reproduction of blood-sucking insects. The bugs are horrendous. They are like pieces of your brain broken free, vibrating violently close to your thin skin, demanding restitution.

"Archery is hell."

"No, hell is a pyjama party in a toaster oven. This is purgatory." Tatyana shoulders her bow expertly. But her aim sucks. She sends arrows hustling wildly into the woods, careening straight up into the clouds and zinging dangerously close to other humans on the range. One of them grazes the branch of a tree next to a mossy stump where Theo and his brother are sitting.

"Can you get that, Kate?" Tatyana calls over her shoulder, already collecting her other misfires.

At Katie's approach, Theo's brother looks up. "I like your bugs," he says, prodding at a glistening banana slug that is nosing its way forward through the mud.

"He likes your insects," Theo agrees, getting up to lift the edge of a rock to expose a riot of potato bugs.

"Right," says Katie, and bends to pick up the arrow, then turns her back on the boys.

Tatyana meets Katie halfway, winks at her. "So?"

"They like our bugs."

"I think they're orphans."

Katie prepares to shoot. She is quite certain her aim is

true, can in fact hear the cushioned splintering sound the arrow will make when it enters the target. The problem is in the letting go. Somehow she always ends up easing the string free, with none of the twanging necessary for a smooth and wilfull trajectory. When she finally releases, the arrow, which is yellow and plastic accented with orange synthetic feathers, falls flaccidly to the forest floor.

"You are *extremely* bad at this." Tatyana is crouched nearby, watching, her sweatshirt pulled up over her head in an attempt to block the bugs.

"Yes," says Katie, only partway glum. "Let's get out of here."

They make a run for it while the counsellor is demonstrating what he claims is an ancient Iroquois bow position. To keep the mosquitos at bay the girls perform rapid karate chops in the air around their faces as they walk. Their breath comes quickly, in urgent puffs. It is unwise to talk in this state.

Back in the cabin, Tatyana reapplies her eyeliner, a fat navy-blue streak across the top lids.

"Even?" She bends close to Katie, her eyes semi-closed like a lizard's.

"Yep."

"Want some?" Tatyana spritzes some cologne on her neck. The room smells of counterfeit roses, deet, and maxi pads.

"Just a bit." Katie offers her wrists.

"Do you think Andy might be on in canoeing?"

Andy is on. He is very on. He gives a thumbs up when he sees them coming over the ridge towards the boathouse, ignores the fact that they are not scheduled to be at the waterfront, sets them both up with paddles: "No shorter than your chin, no taller than your nose."

"I got ya," says Tatyana, which even to Katie sounds pretty sorry.

"OK, Kate?" Andy pokes her in the ribs. She opts for an emphatic nod.

Out on the water, they go to work.

"I like that shirt he's wearing, the way the sleeve's a bit ripped?" Katie is sterning; she switches to J-stroke, points them away from the weeds near the shore.

"Yeah, and excellent hair today, kind of mussed at the front." Tatyana is an erratic paddler; usually she lily-dips distractedly, but there are times when it occurs to her to put some muscle into it. This is one of those times; her paddle is scooping and churning heartily. They are moving at a fast clip out into the open.

Katie wonders if she should tell about the poke. It was a playful tease of a poke, but it hurt a little, and she has filed it in the realm of uninvited tickle. But she wants it to happen again, can imagine it happening again.

"Motorboat," says Tatyana, "stop paddling."

A squat grey-haired woman is helming the motorboat. She raises her hand to the girls as she roars by. They wave back, the canoe peaking and plunging over the wake.

"Did you see Andy's belt?" Maybe there is no need to bring up the poke.

"Mmm, hmm," says Tatyana, trailing her fingers in the waves, "a touch of class." Then, "Do you think he has a girlfriend in the city?"

"Probably. She's probably a waitress." Katie mulls for a moment. "With big tits and a pointy chin," she adds recklessly.

"Yee-aaah." Tatyana is now in full recline in the front of the canoe, and has stopped paddling entirely. "I wish I was a waitress. I wish I was Andy's waitress."

Katie stops paddling too, and gives the boat over to the rock and roll of Georgian Bay, gives herself over to the possibilities spindling out from that statement: *Andy's waitress.*

"Um, might be a good idea to start doing your job there, Skipper." Tatyana is sitting upright, and has actually placed the paddle across her knees in a position of readiness.

It's true; there is some action required of them. They have drifted around the point so that the dock is no longer in sight, and the wind has picked up. Katie turns the canoe around, which takes more vigour and force than she anticipated. Tatyana has set to it with uncharacteristic diligence. They are moving forward, but slowly, the wind bullying them for no apparent reason. They are a bit of a joke, Katie thinks, in this limitlessness punctuated by the spiny protrusions of the Canadian Shield; two girls in a red fibreglass canoe, their lifejackets riding up like puffy straitjackets above their shoulders. She watches the straining in Tatyana's wrist as she pulls the blade of the paddle alongside the gunnel. What is it she notices there? A concentration, yes, but also a restrained jumpiness in the tendons. Fear. Tatyana is scared. And, oh, it frays at Katie's heart to see it. She paddles harder and begins to sing.

> *Go ahead and hate your neighbour, go ahead*
> *and cheat a friend.*

> *Do it in the name of heaven if you can justify*
> *it in the end.*
> *There won't be any trumpets blowing, come*
> *the judgement day.*
> *And on the bloody morning af-tuh-uh-er...*
> *One tin soldier rides away!*

By the time they reach the final verse, they can see Andy, who is bent over just below the tree line, to the left of the dock, singlehandedly tipping the sludge out of one of the rowboats.

> *So the people cried in anger, mount your*
> *horses, draw your swords!*
> *And they killed the mountain people, so they*
> *got their just rewards*
> *There they stood beside the treasure, on the*
> *mountain, dark and red.*
> *Turned the stone and looked beneath it.*
> *Peace on earth ... was all it said.*

They are sad for a moment, and deep into themselves.

"That is a really good song."

"I know." Katie stops paddling. "Do you believe in God?"

Tatyana turns and looks at her. "Once God answered my prayers. But once is not a fan-fucking-tastic record." She pauses for a moment to rearrange the extra lifejacket she has placed as padding under her knees. "And maybe once is not even a record. Maybe it's just once, y'know? I really wish we didn't have to have those powdered potatoes again for dinner."

"Yeah," says Katie, answering a question and a hope.

Because they have completed all the swim levels, Katie and Tatyana have been chosen as assistants to the swim instructor. Mostly, this means suntanning on the dock and blowing the whistle (one long blast) if they see any water snakes in the area. It seems conceited and laughable to Katie that the water has been cordoned off the way it has, the blue and white buoys bobbing ineptly in a line across the cove, a hawk coasting above. It is so different from the pool in the city, which smells of sterility and organization and is divided into two clear sections: the first for the novices and old ladies, who play in the shallows, do a stiff-armed, head-up crawl and throw yellow foam balls into the nets that hang from undersized backboards at either end, the second for the real swimmers in their proud lines, neat within the turbo lanes, who putter and slice, knowing exactly where to go and when to turn, even when they're on their backs. "It's not the heat, it's the humidity," say the old ladies in the change room, standing, stooped and stubborn, in their saggy beige underwear. And the hair dryers hum in the background.

At camp, there are no hair dryers. At camp, the bottom of the swimming area is uneven, unmarked, at times unknowable.

"I thought there might be baptisms," says Katie to Tatyana. "It would be good if there were baptisms."

"Ugh. They force you under, you know."

"Yeah, but when you come up, it's like you're someone else—congratulations!—you're totally transformed."

"I will *never* let anyone push my head underwater." Tatyana snaps the bottom of her bathing suit into place over her butt and passes Katie the suntan lotion.

"I would, I think. I think I would do it."

There is a boy standing underwater. From the dock, Tatyana and Katie can see him. He is not swimming or floating, just standing. Not even moving, but being stirred somewhat by the currents and eddies of the water, his hands waving languidly at his sides, his turquoise swim trunks ballooning around his waist like some alien form of underwater vegetation. But there are no lilies or weeds in the swimming area; he stands alone, without shadow, and although the water is not entirely transparent—tiny bits of the bay hang suspended around him—the lines of his body are clear, only mildly distorted.

"I think that's Theo's brother," says Tatyana, and they both watch as several empty marble-sized balls stream upwards from his mouth like the circles leading to a thought in a comic strip.

Maybe he wants to live down there, is what Katie thinks.

"I think we better tell Sue," is what Tatyana says.

Sue is the swim instructor. She is at the far end of the dock preparing to demonstrate a dive, her toes curled over the edge, chin tucked to chest, head nestled between arms.

"He said he could swim," she says, when Tatyana points. Then again, when she spots him: "He said he could swim."

They stand there, Sue and the girls on the dock, the boy in the water. Until something seizes Sue's features, and she takes a calm uncanny stride from the dock, into the air and down into the cove.

Maybe he wants to live down there. The thought comes again, adamant and elementary. It does not seem a strange thought to Katie—he looked so natural, and only moderately bewitched; more grounded in the water than on the ground.

Sue has pulled the boy up onto the rock that passes for a beach, where he begins to spit and snot, and then to cry. She clutches his head in her lap, holds him like that till she remembers her role, then shakes him free, her hands taking inventory of his body, checking for broken bones, prodding for bruises.

Not likely you'd get bruised under there.

Through it all the boy does not speak, only stares appraisingly up at Sue, his swim trunks now glomming on to his thin legs.

Then Theo is there, wrapping a towel, then his own body, around his brother, enclosing him efficiently.

It says here the sleeping bag should be wrapped in a ground sheet. That it should be waterproof.

Katie watches them, stuck together on the rock like a pair of barnacles. She puts her arm around Tatyana, who leans into her. Before he leads his brother away to the cabin, Theo turns towards Katie and Tatyana and gives an official nod.

"He totally likes you," says Tatyana.

"Whatever." Katie sweeps her gaze along the cliffside on the other side of the cove, above the diving raft, where a sign has been posted. NO CLIFF-JUMPING. Then she scans the murky distance of the water between.

Which is when she sees it, a disturbance near the buoys, a bulge and trail on the surface of the water. She blows the whistle, long and hard, so that Tatyana springs away from her, hands clamped over her ears.

"Snake," she says. "There's a snake."

But, of course, there is no snake. What Katie saw—the clever, quick, limbless creature—is gone. "I think you girls should go get dried off." Sue takes the whistle from Katie's hand.

"No kidding," says Tatyana, and grabs her goggles from the dock.

"Nice colour combo." Tatyana points to Katie's gimp bracelet.

"Uh-huh, how's the cowboy?"

Tatyana is working on a piece of copper tooling. The mould is a man on a horse with a lasso.

"Not great." She holds the copper up to her face to check her lipstick. "Let's get some seed beads and go outside."

On their way out of the craft cabin, they run into Andy.

"Whoa, girls." He holds out a hand, and with the other hand smooths at something below his lip. "Where's the fire?"

"No fire," says Katie, "just seed beads."

"Cool necklace," says Tatyana, and reaches up to touch the wooden beads at his throat.

"Mmm, hmm." He catches her hand in his and rubs his thumb along her wrist. "See you in boating."

"Okay," says Tatyana.

"Bye," says Katie.

The rock outside is grey and fissured, except where it is green with moss, and multi-coloured with bits of colour caught, incongruous, in the cracks.

"Do you think they could ever clean up all of these?" Katie licks her finger and presses it to two tiny beads, a red and a black, then brings them up to her face to examine.

"It would take infinity."

Katie decides to ignore the fact that Tatyana is sniffing at the place on her wrist where Andy's thumb rub happened. "It

doesn't feel like a Saturday today. It feels like a ... a Wednesday."
She pushes down on the moss by her knee. "It's like teeny,
squishy toy trees."

"What?"

"The moss." Katie opens her pill bottle full of beads,
pressing the lid down and to the side. "Childproof," she says,
and pours some of the contents out into the lid, then pulls a
piece of fishing line from her pocket. *Green then two blues then
a yellow. Whole parades of shades.*

"I don't feel like beading," says Tatyana, and lies back on
the rock.

It is hot, and soon, after she has completed six cycles of
colour for her bracelet, Katie lies back too. The day feels like a
really good memory that is somehow happening in the pres-
ent. She closes her eyes and stretches her arms out to the side.

"Y'know those small girls in canoeing?" Tatyana prods
Katie with her foot.

Katie knows. "They're all like *hee, hee, hee.*"

"Mmm," says Tatyana, "the small girls." She lobs the lid
of her pill bottle at Katie.

"Hey." Katie lobs it back.

Tatyana picks it up and holds it in the air above them. The
sun is clear and strong on their faces. "My mom used to make
me help her count her pills. Ever since I was a kid. It was a
game." She places the lid carefully on her stomach, and they
both watch as it rises and falls in time with her breath. "She'd
slide them across the coffee table, one at a time. It's probably
how I learned to count." She grabs onto the lid and places it on
Katie's stomach. "Then she ODed. Code for overdose."

"I know," says Katie, too quickly. *I said it too quickly.*

"While she was in the hospital all these people came over. They made me carry this tray of tiny sandwiches around. They made me carry a fucking tray. And I was the one who counted the pills."

Katie is sweating. "But she's okay now, right?"

"Yep, she's okay. She thinks sending me here will put the fear of God in me."

"Huh. Fear of God." It seems to Katie that God is pretty much the last person anyone should be scared of.

Tatyana is singing to herself, softly.

> *Seek ye first the kingdom of God, and his*
> *righteous-neh-ess*
> *And all these things shall be added onto you*

Katie joins in for the hallelujahs, like an opera star, only with less volume and drama, since it is past lights out.

> *Ah-ley-lou, ah-ley-lou-ou-yah!*

"Yah," Tatyana repeats, "Ah-ley-lou, *yah*." She swings her legs over the side of the bunk.

Katie studies the shape of the feet swinging above her— curvy, with narrow waist-like insteps, and dirty blobs for the pads of the toes, heels and balls, just visible in the light sputtering through the window from the trail.

"Come up here, I really have to tell you something." Tatyana whispers through the space between the bunks.

"Yah," Katie says absently, and pushes on Tatyana's ankle so that her foot balances back and forth.

"I mean, *really*." Tatyana pulls her feet up and dangles her head down instead. "This is major, Katie."

Katie nods and hoists herself up onto the top level like an adolescent bodybuilder, all effort, no decorum.

"Okay," she says, once both her legs have made it, "but I get the wall side. If you get all hyper, you're totally gonna push me out."

"Whatever," says Tatyana, and rearranges herself in showy accommodation. "So what happened is—guess what happened! I made out with Andy! It was so weird, and it just happened while you were in the kybe brushing your teeth ..."

"No *way*. What do you mean you *made out*? What *happened?*" Katie is genuinely pleased and curious, and only feels a light fizz of jealousy at the back of her throat. She knows it is hers too, this making out. It is theirs, hers and Tatyana's, together. She snuggles down on the pillow so that their heads are even, so that the space between them is private and small.

"Well, he was just kind of walking with me towards the cabin, and then he had his hand on my back, well kind of just above my butt, and we just started walking, and he's not really ly talking, and then we just stopped outside the maintenance cabin, and he bends down and his face is all like a nail brush when it touches my cheek, and he's got his tongue in my mouth so I kind of scream, but also stick out my tongue ..." She stops for a second, furrows her brow, and, somehow, her cheeks end up furrowing too.

Katie understands how important it is to get them right, these details, the order of things. She reaches out and twists a piece of Tatyana's hair around her finger in encouragement.

"Yeah, we were frenching for a while. We'll probably sit together at campfire on Sunday. First we frenched, then he touched my boobs. French, boobs, french, boobs ..."

Tatyana didn't really have much in the way of boobs, but she wore clingy shirts, and was a little fat so there was some bumpiness to her. Katie detests her own boobs; they look big even though they're not and she thinks they should be more round, fold over a little. Instead they sit too low on her chest, with their strange puffy nipples that tip skyward like puppies' noses. Most days, she wears a tight undershirt over her bra to flatten them.

"Did he have a boner?" she says, and raises the sleeping bag into the air with her legs, so that her slippery-shod feet touch the rafters.

"Eww, you mean an *erection*?" Sometimes Tatyana could be all The Lady Prissy Superior.

"Congratulations," says Katie, and then they are pitching from side to side, sliding on the narrow mattress, the laughter clasping at them in an unmanageable, marvellous way.

Tatyana is the first to slow her breath, to speak. "I still think Theo likes you." It is an attempt to bolster, to smooth some upset or imbalance between the two girls.

"Whatever, he freaks me out." Katie shoves Tatyana's arm away, with less a laugh than a voiced smile, recycled. Why try to talk about *her,* where is the point in it?

"I heard his parents got shot." Tatyana's face is set in the same expression she uses sometimes while singing hymns, pure and put on. To be solemn so soon after laughter is a trespass. It is bringing Katie down. She suddenly knows she could punch Tatyana square in the nose, can feel the welcome contact, middle knuckle to begging, bull's-eye cartilage.

"Right in front of him. In the middle of the night, they

just bust right in on them. He took his brother and hid behind the dresser. Jenny told me in A&C. Can you imagine?"

"No," says Katie, meaning *I don't want to, don't make me.* "I better go down." She begins the slow clamber to her bed, then stops to waggle her tongue and spasm her groin.

"Fuck *off,*" says Tatyana, and Katie does.

Back on her own bunk, she hunkers down, her back to the world, nose pressed against a graffitied beam. She knows the words scrawled there by heart. *Sex is fun but use pertexion. Jesus loves me the most.* And, inexplicably, *Prince Charles was here and a good time was had by all.* A jagged crown doodled to the side. She has carved her own message above a whorled black knot in the wood: a large letter K, with a plus underneath, and a question mark below that, then a large heart around the whole thing. Who is the question mark? It is up to everyone else to guess. *That's for me to know and you to find out.* She closes her eyes. There are flickering white amoeba against the maroony insides of her eyelids. *Shot.*

Could you imagine it? Could *she* imagine it? If she did, what would happen? When she was younger there were the nightmares, the witches who came roaring, perched high and ridiculous in glistening red tractors. And the trick, when she woke up in a daffy panic, was always to think it through, to think right through to the worst. The *worst.* She'd close her eyes and see it: herself, tied to the railway tracks, paralyzed; the head witch barrelling down the tracks in her tractor. Tracks? Tractor? It didn't matter. It was terrifying. And she would be crushed. This was the worst: the marrow squeezed out of her bones like toothpaste under those giant black rubber treads, her brain a smushed eggplant. And death would be what? Nothing to worry about. A blank. The witches could do as they might, mix her in with the newts and muddy bits of bat. She would feel nothing, be *nothing*.

But to not dream it, to have it there, unfolding in front of you, to the worst. Did it become a dream that you could never think through? *Shot.* And afterward, to not be dead, to live and walk and talk—the dream that was never a dream in the first place dogging you through your nights ...

"Are you asleep?"

"Yes." Katie makes loud snoring noises.

"I'm coming down. Should I bring my nail polish?"

The raid was Katie's idea.

The girls stumble clumsily out onto the trail, pockets bulging, jaws still slack with what they have seen. There is only half a moon in the sky, but it is iridescent and high. Katie's father liked to talk about the moon. "Some people believe the moon was once part of the earth, Kate, that it was flung off when the world was first forming. Now it just hangs out—waiting, waxing, waning, watching—caught in orbit." Katie wants to be in her bed, and she wants to be anywhere but in her bed. In orbit, maybe. *Today is Saturday, and tomorrow is Sunday.*

Tatyana is piecing something together, Katie can tell by the increasing confidence in her stride. *Let's not. It was my idea.*

"Theo's brother," says Tatyana wonderingly, "sleeps with his eyes open."

Sunday mornings at camp are relaxed. The bell does not ring until eight-thirty, and there is sometimes French toast for breakfast. But chapel is serious business. The director, a giddy, God-filled woman, becomes sombre, more director-like. She tells them what they should do, according to the Lord. Then they sing.

> *Jesus is the rock of my salvation*
> *His banner over me is love*
> *Jesus is the rock of my salvation*
> *His banner over me is love*
> *Jesus is the rock of my salvation*
> *His banner over me is love*
> *His banner ... over me-ee ... is love!*

There are actions to the song: a waving motion in the air above their heads on *banner* and a hand placed over the heart on *love*. The director's long necklace swings wide while she sings, then moors itself loyally to one of her large breasts. After the singing is done with, the campers are sent, with their paperback Bibles, to sit on the point and read about Jesus. This will help them prepare a place for Him in their hearts.

Katie and Tatyana find a spot behind a boulder and sit back to back. It is forbidden to talk.

Katie flips through her Bible, then squints up at the sky. The day is a milky-tea colour; clouds steeped in the sun's dull rays and the reflection on the water is causing a slow, slightly stupefying pulse behind her eyebrows. She can feel her friend's rib cage against her own, can sense Tatyana's breathing becoming deep and regular. She fans through the Bible again, then jabs randomly at a page with her finger.

Under Mark, and the sub-heading *A Dead Girl and a Sick Woman*, she finds the following passage:

> He did not let anyone follow him except Peter, James and John the brother of James. When they came to the home of the synagogue ruler, Jesus saw a commotion, with people crying and wailing loudly. He went in and said to them, "Why all this commotion and wailing? The child is not dead but asleep." But they laughed at him.
>
> After he put them all out, he took the child's father and mother and the disciples who were with him, and went to where the child was. He took her by the hand and said to her, *"Talitha koum!"* (which means, "Little girl, I say unto you, get up!"). Immediately the girl stood up and walked around (she was twelve years old). At this they were completely astonished. He gave strict orders not to let anyone know about this, and told them to give her something to eat.

Katie closes the book, sets it down on the rock beside her, then closes her eyes. Grogginess and the glare of the day have made her credulous. They should give the girl porridge, she thinks.

Fire's burning, fire's burning
Draw nearer, draw nearer
In the gloaming, in the gloaming
Come sing and be merry

What is the gloaming, anyway? Katie shifts on the rock. She and

Tatyana have positioned themselves at the edge of the crowd, close to the campfire, so that they can observe the counsellors, but also take off early if things get tedious. Katie is unhappy, though she cannot say exactly why. The campfire is raging and hot, and soon the stars will pierce finely through the blackness above, but the sunset was torrid, the clouds like slabs of bloody meat slapped up against the darkening sky. And there is something irritating about the night closing in around their little circle lit by fire, something duplicitous about this makeshift family.

She feels far away from everything.

And she misses her parents quite utterly. Her father, first thing on a Sunday morning, frying pan in hand: "Sun up, or over easy, little woman? The early birds do not get the tofu, is what I say. Don't tell your mom." They'd sit across from each other, the yellow yolk leaking out onto their plates, their toast spears dripping, and share a cup of coffee. Her mother, in her purple caftan, squatting in the garden: "I want it to look completely chaotic, sweet pea—lots of unplanned variety." She'd toss the seeds in the air and pull Katie in to her breast in a hugging dance, a sweet stain of soil on her cheek, her eyes blank as a baby's. Afterwards Katie would pick up the trowel and straighten things out a little, because too much chaos, she knew, could be a bad thing.

"Jee-sus, the bugs are bad," she exclaims, to keep herself from crying.

Theo, who is sitting a few feet away, deeper in the crowd, looks over at her and frowns.

Who does he think he is, with his tight brown skin and kinky hair?

"Here," says Tatyana, and passes her some Muskol, but does not look at her. She is trying to locate Andy, who does not seem to be among the group at the front.

Katie is going to cry anyway. They are singing the camp-fire song again, this time in rounds. She elbows Tatyana. "What does gloaming mean?"

"Now, *now* is the gloaming," Tatyana says distractedly.

Now is the gloaming.

Tatyana has spotted something in the woods; she has risen onto her knees and is straining to see. Katie also rises up to get a better view. Near the boathouse, two people are standing; the taller one inclined towards the shorter one. Katie recognizes Andy by his bell-shaped Gilligan hat, but she cannot make out the other person. Until the short person lifts her head to kiss the tall person.

"Sue," Tatyana whispers, and rocks back on her heels.

"Are you sure?" But Katie herself is sure. The world is nothing but a big, round fucked up place, all the way from Scarborough to Uganda. She reaches out to her friend.

Tatyana shakes off Katie's hand like a dog shaking off water. Then she grins wide. "They better not make us do that asshole round again."

In the morning, Tatyana will not get out of bed. In fact, she will not move.

"I say onto you, get up," Katie whispers, and places her hand ceremoniously on Tatyana's shoulder.

The shoulder quavers and Katie hears a horking sound

from the vicinity of the head. She bends closer. "Congratulations," she calls softly into the opening of the sleeping bag.

"Do not fucking touch me. And don't let anybody see me. Especially Andy. *Especially* Andy."

"It's just a small bite, I'm sure it will go down soon. You can wear pants."

Tatyana's leg, from the knee down, has ballooned drastically, the skin blotched and generally distressed-looking.

"Probably a spider," the camp nurse had said, while slathering calamine on Tatyana's calf the night before. "Take some antihistamine and rest for a while."

Katie has a hard time believing in calamine lotion; the colour is so phony and it dries like kindergarten paint on the skin. Still, Tatyana had seemed relieved at the time and hobbled heroically back to the cabin.

"You can probably get out of morning dip." Katie strokes the shoulder tentatively.

"I *hate* myself. You don't know anything about me."

You don't hate anybody, not really. You may dislike them strongly, but you don't hate them. Not truly.

"Just leave, please."

"I could bring you some toast."

"Just leave."

Out on the trail, Katie passes several girls from her cabin coming back from the waterfront. She stops one of them. "Did I miss it?"

"Yah, I think Sue left." The girl shakes her head and her towel turban slumps to the side. "You might be able to catch her." She shivers and raises her eyebrows doubtfully.

The reek from the KYBO is particularly bad this morning; the relatively mild aroma of kids' shit undercut sharply by ammonia. Katie hurries past, but the smell follows. It is in her throat. Just before she reaches the lodge, she hears something in the bushes: a rattling. And when she looks, there is movement. A snake? No, only a pile of dry leaves made rowdy by the wind.

At least snakes had the decency to give a warning, and they weren't really evil, no matter what the Bible had to say. Snakes were just *snakes*. And spiders, though sneaky, were also just doing their thing. It was people you had to look out for. They had whole histories and prehistories wrapped up in their heads, whole continents heaving and shifting inside of them that could erupt without warning. Without any warning at all. *Why all this commotion and wailing? The child is not dead but asleep.* And where was Jesus, the pushy, water-walking magician, when you really needed him?

Morning dip is over. There is no sign of Sue, or anyone else for that matter. The sun is poised midway up the flagpole on the point. The wind and water seem friendly, at ease with each other. The morning is glorious. Katie turns to go back to the cabin, shampoo still in hand. At the far, marshy end of the cove, someone is bending towards the water. Katie walks to the trailhead and peers over the woodpile to get a closer look. It is Theo, intent on something bobbing in the waves. She moves closer, pushing her way through clinging brush, her shampoo now wedged in her armpit.

"Good morning, Katie," says Theo, without disturbing his focus on the bobbing thing.

"Morning," she says, and steps out into a narrow muddy

space on the shore.

"I'm trying to save the frog." Theo has extended a long hooked stick above the surface of the water and is now slapping it fitfully just in front of the frog, as if trying to get its attention.

But it is not a frog, really. It is several frogs, Katie thinks, feeding on something, and making a terrible, hungry gasping sound. She squints and steps closer. But where are the heads? She counts six fused legs—or are they tentacles?—two gaping maws, but no distinguishable heads. The freaky not-really-a-frog is spiralling in the water, unable to co-ordinate a kick in any one direction. It is horrifying to watch. Katie brings her hand to her mouth, but does not look away.

"Maybe if you hold on to my hand, I could stretch out ..." Theo is intent on rescue.

Katie shakes her head and gestures towards the creature. "God made that."

Theo glances up at her, then jerks his head towards the horizon. "Then He made that too."

The sky is full of light; the clouds daubed and sectioned with new sun. It sounds silly, but it's the truth: the waves are *dancing* around the rocky shores of the island. For the first time, Katie understands that it is possible to feel two or more completely opposite things at once. She wants very badly to believe and, at the same time, knows that she cannot. And knows that the wanting to believe leaves a gap in her ... In her what? In her soul? It makes her angry: to feel, then to itemize her feelings, then to be no closer to a solution. And because Katie's feelings are sometimes, but not always, played out in her actions, she takes the stick from Theo, leans far over the water and pushes the bungled frog out into the weeds, where it soon becomes tangled and tired of the struggle.

Crickets

Natalee Caple

Hi Sweetheart,

We were talking about you last night at a dinner party. Dad and I were invited to eat with one of the CEOs that he plays golf with. The man was bragging about his son who wants to write a book. Apparently the son is the vice president of ICC (Important Computer Company!) but he has always wanted to be a poet. I gave out your phone number because I thought you could give him some advice and help him get published. I know you got mad the last time I did that, but—I did it anyway!

As to your question what is the central grievance in my life—are you going to write about this? I'm not sure I like the things I say being passed around to strangers. I mean how would you like it if I wrote down somewhere that when you were little you used to walk in your sleep? We found you all around the house in the morning, sleeping on the floor in the kitchen in a closet or at the foot of the stairs. And once our neighbours, the Anstys, called us to say that you were standing in their vegetable garden staring at the cherry tomatoes as if hypnotized. Your dad went to get you, you were like a little zombie in your nightgown and bare feet. He said, Natasha, go back to bed, and you walked home beside him, held his hand and walked upstairs and got under the covers without saying anything. The next day we changed the drop locks to key locks and hung a wind chime on your doorknob. You can write *that* down.

I guess there are a lot of things I would change if I could edit my life. I would get more education. I would have been more ambitious and had an interesting job. As a secretary I always felt like a place marker. But the central grievance in my life? I guess I miss my family. Not my sister (Pip), we've never gotten along and I don't miss Wales, I've gotten used to sunshine. I miss my mother. But I miss my father in a more painful way not only because he's dead but also because I can't remember him very well.

Dad's full name was Percival David Richard Stuart Campbell Probyn. He was a romantic figure in the family because he was always nearby but so impossible to know. When he met Mum they both lived in Cardiff. He was known for racing motorcycles and she had come to watch the races with friends. She was engaged to another boy when they met but Dad proposed to her that first night at a party. They were drinking beer and leaning into each other but not touching. He was leaving to fight the Germans in a week. They spent the whole night talking together. Like two crickets singing in tune they understood each other perfectly. She stayed with him and the party rolled into the morning. Parents became strangely permissive in Cardiff in the days before the young men left to fight, acting against their own Victorian impulses as fascism rushed across the rest of Europe. Perhaps they were thinking of themselves and the nights they lay alone and frightened during the first war, vulnerable in untested flesh.

I think Percy must have exhausted all the words he knew at once that night. No one ever heard him speak at length again. He told young Gwyneth Jones that she had legs like a grand piano and hips like a mountain pony. I think it made her excited to hear a young man talk about her legs and hips even though what he said wasn't nice. I'm engaged, she said at last, afraid to see his face twist with anger.

When are you getting married? he asked.

In a month, she whispered. I'm getting married in a month to a boy I met in school. His name is H— he's sick tonight. I think he'll make a lovely husband. I mean to say I love him.

Well, said Percy, I'm leaving in a week. I'm going to fly fighters against the Germans. I don't think I'm coming back. You can marry me first and marry him after I'm dead.

I'll have to think about it, whispered Gwyneth Jones, feeling suddenly ordinary and unsure. I can't decide. I'll need a few days. You should meet my family. I'd have to buy a dress.

Wear this dress, he said. I like this dress.

She cried as she confessed to her fiancé. She shook her head and tears flung from her cheeks, a few drops landed on his hands. He listened numbly, his jaw fell lower, a deep furrow sliced his smooth forehead. She made the mistake of defending her case, describing her infidelity as a kind of romantic nationalism saying, Percy Probyn was about to leave every-thing behind, risk everything, to spit in face of the enemy. Show the world how powerful and wild were the hearts of the Welsh, and all for the sake of the *English,* those ingrate bull-dogs—but we *must* stop fascism! she exclaimed, pounding a fist on her knee.

Her abandoned man could not listen. Gwyneth, you idiot, he said. We're all going. In a month you won't see a man in Cardiff. He doesn't know he'll die, no one knows which of us will die. We'll all be there but he'll have your photograph, and he'll have you.

Gwyneth was shocked into silence. Finally she responded to him. I've never seen you look so cruel, she said. I've done something terrible, haven't I?

Gwyneth Jones and Percy Probyn married after four days, and then after seven days he went away to fight overseas. He took risks. He flew with the confidence of someone who has decided to die. But he didn't die. He became a war hero. He was part of the Desmond unit in France, which guided British planes by radar. When his airfield base was being bombed he stayed behind alone after the evacuation and ran the radar to guide the other fighters through the night and through the shelling to safe landings. He was given the British Empire Medal for his bravery.

So there you have it—he was a motorcar racer and a war hero. He was a man's man and a ladies' man, but he wasn't much of a daddy. Family life was alien to him.

He didn't understand children. He and his sisters had been brought up in separate boarding schools and as children left alone with children they always thought of themselves as adults. Whatever pale memories he retained of familial intimacy could not compete with the brightness of his late adolescence. As a father he was impossible. He didn't play with Pippa and me or talk to us much at all. His face seemed miles away. He smiled, a lot, but I can't call back his laugh. I followed him around like a dog but everything he liked to do he liked to do alone. He was an amateur photographer. He was always taking pictures of us, always behind a camera. We were on the beach, chasing crabs with our fingers in the water. We were sipping tea in a café at Hay-on-Wye. We were in the fields surrounded by sheep. We were in our beds asleep. And he was there, behind the camera, with us and not with us. Then he'd go into the darkroom and be in there all day hidden by the smelly mysterious darkness, behind a lightproof door. I sat outside with my shoulder against the closed door, my head against the wood as I read my comics and listened to him walk around, lift invisible objects, shift things and shuffle papers.

When at last he came out I fell backwards against his feet. I did it every time so he would pick me up with his hands under my arms and set me on my feet before he moved away again. The smell of the chemicals on his hands and in his clothes was so strong my eyes filled up with tears. In the room behind him a clothesline was hung over a table lined with cans and tubs of developing fluid. Along the clothesline, pictures of Mum, and me, and Pippa were held aloft with wooden pegs.

He liked to work on his car in the garage. I remember one day when Mum gave me sandwiches and tea to bring to him. I struggled to balance the heavy pewter tray and the teacup rattled on the saucer. He was leaning over the engine under the hood. His hands were black with grease. He lifted his head from under the hood and smiled and gestured at me to leave the tray on a chair. Then he ducked back under the hood again. Daddy, I said out loud at last. He stopped working and looked up at me. What is it, Patricia? he asked, controlling his irritation. I thought for a minute for something to say. Daddy, there's a sale on tools at Foster's, I called out at last.

Thank you, Patricia. I'll go over there later when I'm finished here.

Do you want me to hold your sandwiches for you? I asked, sensing that I was about to be dismissed. Your hands are covered in grease.

No thank you, Patricia. That isn't necessary. I can feed myself. And with that he re-entered his world and I was abruptly left in mine.

He also liked to garden in his greenhouse at the bottom of the garden. The greenhouse was filled with tomato plants and lettuce, cucumbers and any vegetable you could grow on a vine. It was like a little jungle all hot and steamy inside and smelling like fresh-tilled earth. I watched him through the glass moving around and it was like he was in another country, a country where it didn't rain except on the plants, where it never got drafty at night, and where your footsteps were silenced by the soft moss on the flagstones. I might have been watching him from a thousand miles away. He never looked up from what he was doing.

If I had stayed in Wales after I married I would have learned how to talk to him. He just didn't understand children. He did love me, it was apparent in the careful way he spoke and moved around when I was there. He wasn't antisocial and he wasn't cold, exactly. Pip got to know him well once she became an adult. He and Mum shared a bed until he died at eighty-one. He was a man, not a trace of boy about him. But he was a nice man, a quiet man. An entirely private sort of person. I was angry that he never came to Canada to see me or you once you were born. We were always returning to him. But, if I were less self-involved in my twenties, or less involved with you girls in my thirties, I might have got to know him better. But then again, maybe we were always too different to be close. I loved him, he was my father, but maybe he could see from his adult point of view that we really had nothing in common and I was just too small to understand.

Anyway, Love you,

Mum

My mother's father was so distant he's more like a fictional character to me than like a person I once knew. In every memory I have of him he is leaving the room. It's strange to think of him as the eager would-be soldier seducing my grandmother into marriage overnight. Or as the hero who ran back between exploding shells to save his compatriots one awful night during the war. It's strange and yet it makes sense. He so liked being alone that he may have felt the space around him expand in the stuttering darkness. The bombs exploded the tarmac; the pilots' voices crackled over the radio waves. The planes appeared as discreet blips of light moving across a screen. And he was finally able to protect those precious bodies from a distance.

I have one of the medals he won racing motorcycles. It's made of white and red gold and shaped like a shield; I have it on a silver chain. On the front M.M.C. is engraved. Master of Motor Cars maybe? On the back it reads *Goss Hall Grass Race / P. Probyn / 21/7/29*. Six years before the day Gwyneth J's fiancé began to sneeze and wheeze and backed out of an afternoon with friends. And she went on without him, excited about her new bathing suit, which revealed a fraction of thigh white as refined sugar. She and her friends posed for each other, brownie cameras like black magic boxes held in turn by one while the others clambered onto the rocks by the shore and threw arms around shoulders, kissed each others cheeks and smiled. Their hair in the pictures in still neatly curled in spite of the waves. Hair spray in Wales is strong enough to hold up buildings after dynamite.

Gwyneth's eyeglasses are speckled with mist. She has her hands on her hips and one thigh is turned outward to show the daring swimming suit. Black because it's slimming, cut with a round neck that shows her collarbones.

Later someone suggested the grass races. The bikes were grey with dried mud. The smell of oil hung in the air. All the riders looked the same under their helmets and goggles. But one pulled ahead of the others, tilting as he rode as if he had no thought to right himself, he did not care if he crashed, he was not afraid of falling. Who's in the lead? she asked her friend. Percy, her friend answered. Percy Probyn always wins.

I wonder what it was like that first night they were married. Lying in bed together in silence, smear of icing on his cheek.

The windows open to the damp night. Crickets whispering. The other guests and residents of the Angel Inn moving in the hallway. His hands on her skin touching her arms and legs and back and breasts. Stroking between her legs and then entering her. How she might have held onto him.

I've forgotten some of your names, she might have said, still unnerved. One day he doesn't exist and she has never been totally naked in bed before and then within a week he is her husband, her strange husband with a half-dozen names, and he will be leaving her by the time the weekend is over. How to negotiate her tiny world now that it has been invaded by sex and maybe by love. Is it love?

They were in love in their seventies. I watched her touch his shoulder, touch his arm whenever she passed him in the room. And he reached back to grip her fingers. At seventy she performed in drag in the pantomime playing the king, wearing a velvet crown and a felt cape over the shirt and pants she borrowed from her husband. I sat beside him in the darkened theatre. He never turned his head or spoke, he simply stared at her until the curtain fell. He thought he would die in France or over Berlin. He did not dream of domestic bliss or of fussing with his car or sorting out his children or attending to his familiar wife in bed. He did not dream of my mother and he did not dream of me. He may have been too honourable to come right out and say to Gwyneth Jones that what he wanted was to have sex before he died and so he proposed, thinking heroic thoughts of nuptial orgasms followed by a fiery plane crash. Maybe she shared his fantasy. To come and then to go. To lie in bed and really know someone naked in the dark, someone that you had spent only breathless days speaking to and barely a kiss before facing death. Her first engagement was to a man she thought would make a good husband, a good father, her partner for life. Her second engagement was to a man who made her legs shake when he told her she looked like a Welsh mountain pony—stocky and feisty. Picture her, a young woman at a party with a beer in her hand breathing in the dusky scent of men and feeling like a mountain pony climbing a steep green range, skin letting off steam in the rain.

Book of Lies

Suzanne Matczuk

THE LUCICH GIRLS were born liars. They were liars on their father's side, just like they were Hungarian on their father's side. But they did not all lie. Giulia would if she could but she was never very good at it. Stella did not, or, more accurately, would not. For Lily, lying was second nature.

The Lucich girls were different as could be. Giulia helped in the bakery, Lily sang in a nightclub, and Stella gave herself to God. Not like the boys in the war who gave themselves to God—she wasn't dead or anything—she lived in the nunnery up the mountain behind the town. She left when Giulia was thirteen, which was fine with Giulia because then Giulia got a bed to herself. Soon after that Lily climbed out the window and never came back and Giulia got her own room.

Lily wasn't Lily's real name. It was Eleanora. But the way she saw it, it was up to everyone to decide their own stories for themselves. People who denied themselves opportunities for personal revision showed not only a lack of imagination in Lily's books, but a true lack of character. At the nunnery, Stella's name was Sister Maria Teresa. Giulia said that technically, that counted as personal revision. Lily disagreed. As Stella had not come up with it herself, she was disqualified.

Giulia considered herself an anthropologist of untruth. Every lie she heard or told she marked down in a little book she carried with her in her skirt pocket. From experience, Giulia knew that lying was not easy. There were many subtleties to appreciate, skills to hone, and situations to assess. The timing of the lie was important, for one thing, as was the believability of the lie, the gullibility of the subject and the sincerity of the performance.

Giulia experimented with many types of lies, but never quite mastered any of them. She started with the most basic kind of lie—the kind you would tell a five-year-old. When her mother's friend Signora Midoro came into the shop with her little Carlo, Giulia would offer to take him for a walk. Carlo was a good subject. He was eager to believe that his shoulder was his elbow, the sea was made of fish pee and "to scurry" meant to eat a lot of cheese. But he had an innate skepticism about any lies involving sheep or goats, no matter how clever, and after awhile she gave up.

Her sisters proved more difficult. Stella was not a good subject, as she believed everything that Giulia told her. Lily was not a good subject either, as she never believed anything that Giulia told her. Her parents were much more unpredictable and interesting, but after lying about visiting a sick girl who up and died shortly thereafter, which almost landed Giulia in quarantine, Giulia decided that lying was not for her and she abandoned the pursuit.

She did, however, continue to document all manner of untruths in her Book of Lies. The lie about the sick girl went under the category of "Lies That Backfire." Other categories included "Basic Experimental," "Harmful Experimental" (she had no stomach for this category herself, but noted incidents she had heard of), "Harmless" (flattery, empty compliments), "Collaborative" (to help Lily, for example), "Backfire Collaborative" (Lily tells her own lie without consulting Giulia and they both get caught), "Compound" (where one lie necessitates another lie, which necessitates another lie, and so on; this category is always cross-referenced with "Backfire"), and "Unintentional."

Also, in the first few pages of the book, as a sort of introduction, she wrote out the story of the fourteen liars, as told to her by her uncle Kaz, who knew everything about the town of Fiume, which is where they lived:

This Book belongs to Giulia Lucich, Direct Descendent of Tas Lucich (Great-Great-Grandfather) Captain of Industry and Liar, one of the Fourteen.

Simeon Adami came to Fiume in 1785, back when Fiume was still a village. He was a rich man from the farthest reaches of the Empire. He was known to have good luck with business and he kept to himself. Soon enough he was so rich and so lucky people started to talk. They said he had allegiances. They said he was in league with something so unspeakable and so dark that old women made the sign of the cross when they passed him on the street. One day Simeon Adami was digging at a shrubbery, as Simeon Adami was partial to his own gardening, when his shovel struck something in the ground. It was buried treasure. This a kitchen servant could see, watching from a window.

Simeon Adami dug up that treasure and carried it to his study, locked the door and kept the key on his person. Soon the whole town was in a state of agitation. What was this treasure, they wanted to know. And why did Simeon Adami not come forward and offer a portion of the treasure to the town, as a gesture of good will. He offered not even a florin. Suspicion grew pitched, and soon turned mean. Police let rumours settle into deep fester and then started their investigation, which was knocking on Simeon Adami's door, taking him under arrest and throwing him in jail. They let him stay in the jailhouse until they had gone about the town and rounded up 14 respectable citizens who would testify in court. There was a naval officer and a merchant, a governess and a tailor, and various other gentlemen and ladies including Tas Lucich, Captain of Industry. They all swore to Simeon Adami's partaking in a whole list of crimes, all of them not true. The son of Simeon Adami went to the capital to request an appeal, but by the time the emperor declared Simeon Adami free Simeon Adami was in the jailhouse two years. The people of Fiume thought Simeon Adami would pack up his treasure and move on after his release. But he did not. He built a big long house with 14 windows looking onto the canal. Under each window he stood a column, and on top of each column he placed a bust. Each bust was a likeness of a citizen who had testified against him in court. There were 14 in all, one for each citizen. They were called the Fourteen Liars, and each day for one hundred years the liars stood on their pedestals along the Fiumara, staring out at the people in the street. One day the liars were moved to the grounds of the Archduke's Summer Villa, across from the Court of Justice, and that is where they are to this day.

Underneath the text there was a note written as an afterthought:

There was no buried treasure. It was nothing but a few broken pots and bits of carved jade. Not surprising as Simeon Adami lived so close to the ruins of Solin. The treasure was worth nothing.

Tas Lucich was the Lucich girls' father's grandfather. The girls' father's name was Kòsa Lucich, which is about as Hungarian as it gets. But the advantage to being a liar is being able to overrule any aspect of one's history at one's convenience. As a result Kòsa Lucich had chosen to overlook his Hungarian-ness and embrace his Italian-ness, even though he did not have a drop of Italian blood in him. To be fair, this was common practice in Fiume, and one did not need the excuse of being a genuine liar to undertake such fancy. Most of the well-to-do, regardless of blood, considered themselves Italian. It was a state of mind more than anything else. Being Italian meant the good things in life. It meant being all for opera, fancy cakes, itinerant poets, grandiloquent drama, and imported perfume. It was not fashionable to be Hungarian. Being Hungarian meant tedious administration and meddlesome government practice. And it was never fashionable to be Slav. The Slavs lived on the other side of the Fiumara River, over in Susak. They worked in the factories and the shipyards and the docks. Kòsa's mother was, in fact, Croatian, but as far as he was concerned that was a fact hardly worth mentioning.

The girls' mother's name was Rosa Lucich, née Rosa Carboni, and she really was Italian. She worked hard to run the family bakery and café. Her husband spent most of his time at the wine shop across the street with his Italian Nationalist friends, shouting and banging the table tops with his fists.

After Stella and Lily had gone, Giulia stopped going to school and started helping Rosa. She would get up in the middle of the night and shuffle down the stairs to the hot bakery kitchen where her mother would be stoking fires and shaking flour into great bowls. Her mother taught her how to knead the bread dough and let it rise and form into white pasty loaves, then how to push the loaves into the blazing ovens on wooden paddles. While the bread was baking they would start on the pastry dough, roll it into thin delicate sheets. While the pastry was baking the woman who came to help bake the cakes started mixing up the batter, and while the cakes were baking they would start on the custards and crème brulées. It was hard work, especially the bread. Giulia didn't think she could do it. Her little fingers ached and cramped, her small wrists bent to and fro like willow boughs, and sharp pains shot up her forearms. But after a time she got the muscle for it, and mother and daughter worked side by side like old friends.

Giulia had little time away from the café, but when she did, she went for long walks by herself. She walked up and down the Corso, along the Dead Canal, along the harbour front, through the public gardens, through the narrow streets of the old city, and through the parks that looked down over the town. She especially loved the grounds of the Archduke's summer villa. He had been a passionate botanist, and the garden was full of exotic oriental plants, cypresses, laurels and jades, all of which thrived despite the rocky karst ground.

The garden also housed the busts of the Fourteen Liars, and Giulia spent many hours crouched there, staring at their worn and pitted faces. There was no mistaking her great-great-grandfather Tas Lucich. The likeness to her own father was uncanny—same long nose, same narrow chin, same close-set eyes. Later on, when she was home, she would stare at her own face in the mirror, comparing each detail of her features to those of her great-great-grandfather.

One day she opened the Book of Lies and wrote down the title of a new section. She called it "Legacy of Liars," and she marked the busts down as they stood left to right and numbered them one to fourteen. Under number eight she wrote "Tas Lucich—Captain of Industry." As for the rest—well, the town must be full of their descendents. She likely saw them every day, in the café, at the market, on the street, at the church on Sunday mornings. She studied the busts long and hard, memorized their every feature, and then went about the town in search of their resemblance.

This new obsession exasperated Rosa.

"Giulia!" her mother would scold. "Stop staring at the customers."

"Sorry, Mama, I can't help it," Giulia would say.

"Yes, you can," her mother would reply. "Stop this right now. The liars are dead and gone. Let them alone why don't you."

One day a boy came into the café who Giulia had never seen before. He had close-cropped curly black hair and shy eyes with long lashes. Giulia stood at the table and looked at him hard, as was her custom. She stared at the soft lines of his nose, the round smoothness of his cheeks, the surprised arch of his brows. He looked down at the table. When he looked up she still stared.

"Well?" she said. "What can I get you?"

"A limonata," he mumbled, and when he was done he left the money on the table as he could not bring himself to say another word.

He started coming into the café often. He worked his way up to being able to order pastry and coffee, and after a time he was asking how she was doing. One day he asked her name.

"Giulia," she said as she walked past. She cleaned some tables, walked around behind the counter and took some orders. He was standing up to leave when she walked past him again, stopped and turned around.

"What's yours."

"Giovanni Rinaldi." His gaze shifted to the floor.

"How come I've never seen you before?"

"My father was transferred. From Milan."

"What does your father do?"

"He's a manager at the torpedo factory. They needed more. Managers. Production has been up, you know. Since the war."

"Yes, of course," she said, and walked away.

One day Giovanni asked Giulia to go for a walk.

"Ask my mother," Giulia said.

"I don't want to go for a walk with your mother. I want to go for a walk with you."

Giulia gave him a sharp look, then smiled.

"Giulia, I don't know anything about you," he said as they walked together up the Corso. He took small steps, trying to match her stride. They had been silent since they passed the Filodrammatica.

"My name is Giulia."

"I know that much."

"I work in a bakery."

"I know that too."

"I'm Italian."

He nodded.

"I'm a liar."

Giovanni stopped and looked at her.

"You don't look like a liar."

"It's funny you should say that."

They were engaged to be married in the winter, a few months before Italy entered the war. One day in June, Giulia found herself standing with Giovanni on the dock. They were surrounded by crowds of young men on their way to sign up, their families and friends, sweethearts and wives gathered around in varying states of anxiety, excitement and despair, waiting to wave goodbye.

Giovanni kissed Giulia on the cheek and she took his hand.

"Goodbye," he said.

"No," she said. "Not goodbye."

And then she told him two lies, although she did not know it at the time. The first was "I'll see you again." The second was "I love you."

She discovered the first to be a lie when Giovanni's father showed up at the café one day with his hat in his hands. Giovanni had been killed at the Tyrol along with 120 other soldiers. They had been killed in an avalanche. Giulia thanked him for telling her and then she walked down the stairs to the bakery kitchen. She sat for a long time thinking of her fiancé, dead under a white blanket of snow.

She discovered the second to be a lie when she first saw Valente. Never had she seen a face like his. It was all planes and angles, perfectly put together like he had been drawn by Leonardo da Vinci, a sketch for one of his perfect machines. And when she stood at the table and stared, as was her custom, he looked up and stared right back. His eyes were dark and mocking. This time it was she who could not find the words.

She set the coffee and the brandy down with shaking hands. He touched one of her hands with his and said *Grazie,* and she knew she was lost.

One morning in spring she sat alone in the bakery kitchen watching the loaves bake in the oven. She pulled the Book of Lies out of her skirt pocket and opened to the page that said "Unintentional." She marked down the two lies she had told Giovanni. She hesitated, then marked down the two she had told herself. The first was "Valente loves me." The second was "Everything will be fine." She closed the book and threw it in the fire. She watched it flare up and die down. The flames licked at the pages of the book like tongues until the paper curled up black and there was nothing left.

Floating Bob's Dreams
Christy Ann Conlin

thirty

Back fat. I can't stop feeling the back fat. So I ask my husband.

    –What about the back fat?

He's having a pee.

    –Like bacon you mean?

    –No, I say. Like back fat. I mean back fat. On me.

He squints in the candle light.

    –Like bacon fat? On you? On your back?

    –No. Like do I have fat on my back? Can you see it there?

He sighs, rolls his eyes, shakes a few drips and leaves.

    From the tub I can hear magazine pages turn in the living room as he calls from the couch.

    –Will you come out and stay on the boat this weekend? I don't have to work.

    The boat has recently been moored on the river. Bob is

working up there for a few months and had someone bring the boat out. The plan is for me to commute so we don't have to be apart. And he says we don't have to be apart (if I'm being kind) which means I smile a lot (because that's being kind, right?). I can study on the boat. I can come whenever I want (when he invites me). Like the last place, up North above the tree line, where I sat alone while he worked, except when Martelle, his colleague, would have me for tea, would take me to the greenhouse to look at flowers, or when the three of us would have dinner. But I don't want to go. I dread it. Because of the boat—it's falling apart. But I don't tell him that. He loves the boat. He loves to talk about sailing. In my head I wonder why he doesn't go sailing but I just smile and nod while I hum inside, *mmmmmmm*. He thinks that because I'm from the East Coast I've got the sea in my blood—he grew up surrounded by land and so I bring authenticity to the sailing passion. I think, *the only goddamn way the sea will be in my blood is if we sink in your goddamn boat, my man.*

I'm heading naked for the bath with my nose full of lavender when I see the letter on the table, sitting on the orange flowered cotton tablecloth. It's material Bob pulled out of a sail bag from his one trip, smelling of mildew, his favourite smell. I smiled, sniffed and washed it when he left, sending the mildew down the drain.

The boat smells like mildew. It smells like mildew and diesel fuel and kerosene and Bob says a real sailor smells just like that. It gives me the willies because he's got big plans for the boat and me, he says, though so many of his big plans just fall apart. Plans so detailed I know they were made before me, not because of me or with me, and the plans will go on after

me and I know this but I hum inside my head so I don't have
to think about that, *mmmmmmm.*

The letter sits in the centre of the centre flower. I ask if
there is any more mail. Silence. He turns the page. *No.*

I leave wet fingerprints on the envelope. Tracy. My mother
must have given her my address.

seventeen

Seventeen with pink cheeks standing there in a strapless bra
and curled hair. Tracy's helping me dress before Adam comes
to get me in his father's car. I put on the hot pink lipstick to go
with the big taffeta Cinderella dress and black patent-leather
heels. I love the dress. I'm a hot babe.

–Back fat.

–What?

–You've got back fat.

–What do you mean, back fat?

–Fat.

–Where?

–Idiot. On your back. You've got fat on your back.

–I do not.

–Yes you do. Everyone in my family has it. All the girls.
But we've got perky tits. Yours sag.

Tracy hauls her sweatshirt up and they might as well be
growing off her collarbone. And she is covered in back fat.
She's like a walrus on a rock. But I don't have back fat and I
say

–I don't have back fat.

She smiles.

–Sure you do. And saggy tits.

I'm seventeen and even if they don't grow out of my collarbone I know they still aren't sagging because I'm only seventeen.

–*Warner's Super Support, Wonder Bra Full Lifter, Daisy Full and Firm.*

She reels them off like we're at a square dance.

–And get the girdle pants. For the back fat.

–Girdle pants?

–Yeah. Slim and trim. Holds in back fat. No one will know unless they grab you really hard.

She smiles and waits. I hate her guts but I don't pout this time. She can keep waiting. I grin like I'm in agreement about back fat and saggy tits and continue to smile and hate her guts for the next ten years.

thirty

Sitting on the bus out to Bob and the boat. The mid-autumn sun is twisted in the sky. Like blubber. Orange and red blubber twisted in the glorious evening sky. I peek out the window at the mountain peaks dipped in snow and I feel nothing. Where is the splendour of nature, I wonder. I've got the letter in my knapsack. The letter from Back Fat. What does she want from me?

Bob is waiting at the station, dirty, with bags the colour of tea under his eyes. I can smell hamburger on his breath. The boat waits in an industrial park. I can't believe it. This is where he expects me to live? This is where I'm going to write my thesis? We are walking there. No car. How can he just head out to sea if he has a car? he says. I open my mouth and say, *back fat.* I'm losing it. Bob looks at me and I say, *I mean wonderful.* He shakes his head and I smile.

We walk in silence through the industrial park, past a cedar mill. The marina is tucked down a steep embankment on the river so the industry is hidden. In my mind I imagine rolling down the embankment, plopping in the water and floating away like a log. A free log.

When we walk down the dock and I see the *Snapper,* I say, *oh she looks gorgeous,* though her paint is peeling, the teak is rotting and the sails haven't been raised in months—I'm thinking these days it's like a mobile home at dock. I say it once and Bob glares at me, I've jarred the dream. The boat is made of ferro cement and if it can float, I think maybe anything can.

It's really quiet on the dock. Like so quiet that murderers and killers could be waiting behind every pole and mast. Bob says there's one other couple living down here. He points to the boat beside us. A warm light burns deep inside.

We go inside the *Snapper.* It's all toasty from a little space heater and Bob lights the kerosene lamp. It would be cozy but it stinks—the little sink is full of dishes, slimy and abandoned. I've known Bob to just throw them out and buy new—when company is coming. But at least it's warm. I sit down in the salon and a plate sticks to my ass. I look around at the books on the shelves, and at the mahogany galley where Bob is busy cooking up spaghetti. I can see the moon out the little portholes shining silver on the river and the snow of the mountain.

Being in a sailboat is like being in love. On a good day, it's the coziest, safest and most exciting thing to be in; on a bad day it's like a coffin with standing room.

The boat rocks gently all night long. I listen to Bob snore and pull the dirty sheets closer to me—there is a vague comfort in the smell of his stale sweat. I lie there all night, just in case the boat breaks free and starts floating down the river. I'll be able to get Bob up in time to rescue us. The perils of sailing are as real moored to a dock. They're just different.

It's noon and we drink coffee and read the paper in a diner. I'm taking the four o'clock bus back to the city to do some work because Bob has been beeped. He has to work the night shift tonight. He says he forgot and I smile. We used to fight all the time until I got good at the smiling thing.

But I'm not taking the afternoon bus because there is no bus, Bob got the time wrong. We find this out after standing by the bus stop for thirty minutes in the rain. I ignore him and look in the gutter while Bob says things like this happen. A guy he works with drives by, rolling down his window. The last bus went at noon and the next one goes at 7 A.M. I smile as the rain hits my face.

Bob makes phone calls while I sit on the curb soaking up the raindrops. Picking my thumbnail, I listen to him tell me his friend Pete will pick me up and take me to a concert at the high school. And then I can go back to the boat and he will be there in time for breakfast. I say nothing. He asks me to try to be positive. This is my job, being positive.

seven

I'm seven years old on a mandatory Sunday visit with my parents to family friends in this trailer court. My father sits there nervously counting my mother's drinks while I watch her light smoke after smoke. The family friends show slides of old people. There are no other kids and the afternoon drones on and on and on until I can't stand it anymore so I run out the door and down the street. I get lost among the rectangles these people call home and slide my new red coat down a white vinyl wall. I cry, thinking about my good-smelling room. I know where everything is there. My mother finds me shivering and says I have to be a polite girl or else or else or else. From then on, I hide in the backyard every Sunday until they stop forcing me into the car. I swear I won't ever go anywhere I can't leave, and it will take years to realize that I grew up and broke the oath, that was the real betrayal.

thirty

I'm sitting in the boat. I'm sitting there looking at all the books but I can't read them because I'm on guard duty. A knock. I stand up and the lantern swings. The slightest motion rocks the *Snapper*. Pete yells hello and I slide back the hatch.

We jump in his shiny blue Mercedes and zoom off for the high school. The concert is sold out. He's at least fifty and I wonder if he likes babysitting his colleague's partner. We go to this restaurant and I have no idea where I am except that it's some built-up sprawl of a once-small town. We pass huge churches with neon crosses, fast-food restaurants, malls that seem to repeat every mile, townhouse complexes. I could never navigate my way out of here; I'm at his mercy. He's a nice guy though and we talk about herb treatments and evangelical Christians, all the places Bob has worked and I've visited, the people who look after me when Bob works, who make me tea, take me out for dinner.

Pete walks me back to the boat, telling me it's dangerous down here at night. I know it's dangerous, he doesn't need to tell me this. The light is on in the houseboat beside the *Snapper* so at least I feel a bit better, though they must just be sitting in there meditating as I haven't seen a person in or on the boat. Pete asks me if I've done a self-defence course. I say no but I'm really confident. I've got padding. I've got back fat, I think. He tells me he's done Tai Chi and it has made him strong. I say, yeah. His face is yellow under the dock lights and he looms there like a post. He can throw someone twenty feet. Can knock them down and stop their heart. Just like that. He smiles softly. Great, I say. He stands there grinning, saying we must get together again. I say I'll be in the city a lot for the next couple of weeks. Years, I think. I climb aboard the boat, waving. He stands there all jaundiced. So I open the lock, slide back the hatch and wave again. He's still standing there. Goodnight, I call. Goodnight, he calls. I pull the hatch shut. But he doesn't go anywhere.

twenty-eight

July, and I fly into Kentucky from Vietnam. I've been teaching

Buddhist nuns English and now I'm in the USA to rest and relax with my friend Gail from high school. Her husband is in Moscow for the summer, learning languages. We think it will be a good time for a long visit. We will drive home together and she will visit with her family and I will head off to university.

Saigon-San Francisco-Chicago-Lexington and there is Gail all tanned and summery. In the car she tells me Tracy is flying in next week. She's going to drive back with us. I'm quiet, she's quiet and then she says she's sorry, Tracy just announced she was coming, she had even bought a ticket. She's taken a month off from her shoe store in Toronto and was just in Finland for two weeks. She hated Finland but heard it was the place to be.

All the way through Kentucky-Ohio-West Virginia-Pennsylvania-New Jersey-New York-Connecticut-Massachusetts-New Hampshire-Maine-the ferry crossing of the Atlantic to Nova Scotia-the drive down highway 101 to Nolan I write in my journal.

I hate the person in the back seat.
I hate the person in the back seat.
Die Die Die.
Die Die Die.
Tracy says she wishes she could have my inspiration and write so much.

Gail's the only one insured to drive the car so Tracy and I are always the passengers. Whenever I want to sit in the back, she does. Whenever I want to sit in the front, she does. If we stop for a break and I want to take a walk, she comes. When I read a book, she asks which one. She wants to listen to commercial radio and we want to listen to tapes. She talks inces-

santly about how great dried herring is and the unknown
delicacies of Finnish cuisine.

At the washroom stop on the Interstate, Gail rolls her eyes.
She can't believe Tracy. I'm furious and ask why she let her
come along. She feels bad—doesn't know why she said yes.
Sorry. And I'd like to run into the woods.

We go back out to the car and Tracy is leaning on the car
between the front and back doors. She asks me where I want
to sit. I smile and say the back and she says that's where she
was going to sit. I open the door anyway and get snug, leaning
on the cooler with my feet out the window. Gail runs back to
the washroom for paper towel and Tracy leans in the window.
Why do I always have to have my own way? I shake my head and
shut my eyes. Maybe she will explode. She wears a unitard
under all her clothes, to slim her body.

We stop in Boston for the evening. We have no reserva-
tion and end up in a ritzy hotel room at $250 a night. Tracy
grabs a bed for herself, saying Gail and I can share. Gail takes
a shower and comes out in lacy underwear. Tracy whistles and
Gail looks at her. Tracy looks at me and says it's just that we're
too fat too wear stuff like that. I'm not fat, I say, however I
can't bring myself to say, BUT YOU ARE.

Nova Scotia and I am so glad to get out of the car I don't
even look at Tracy. They drop me off at my parents house and
I wave goodbye breathing a sigh of relief. The relief chokes up
when I am in the sun at the beach two days later and Tracy
waddles over. I'm leaving for Vancouver in a few days, I tell
her, and so I have to relax now. *That's fine with old Tracy,*
SHE'LL JUST SIT THERE AND READ A BOOK.

And it's the book I was reading in the car. I tell her this and she acts surprised. I just lie there in the sun and wish I was already heading west. And I want to scream, *go home go home go home,* and let all my air out but I don't. I suck in more and wonder if I will implode.

thirty

So Pete is still standing out there on the dock. His black shoes like beetles outside the porthole. There's no phone on board and no gun. My life is over. I sit down at the table and make a plan. I'll start the boat. Right. The wheel and the throttle are outside so the boat will be running but it will be tied to the dock with the engine going and us not escaping. I'm thinking about the boat as my companion now, something I'm responsible for. The shoes are still there. I look through a drawer in the galley and pull out a knife. Armed.

The waves lap against the side of the boat and I hear the shoes click away. I peer out a porthole on the dock side and see Pete tall and thin like Anthony Perkins in *Psycho.* He walks up the gangway and over the main wharf.

I'm alone. The clock says eleven. Ten hours until Bob's return. It's ten hours that won't end. I know this at the start. I grab a book. *The Strange Last Voyage of Donald Crowhurst,* a reconstruction of a journey, a journey of many kinds. It is based on the logbooks of Donald Crowhurst, a competitor in the first single-handed non-stop round-the-world sailboat race in 1968, the *Sunday Times* Golden Globe.

Crowhurst

Donald Crowhurst was desperate to prove himself, very proud. He was an inexperienced sailor (as far as being prepared for zooming around the world alone), out at sea in a poorly prepared boat, the *Teignmouth Electron*. His boat was an early trimaran that should have been covered in fibreglass but because of time pressures and delays, the plywood deck was covered with a coat of paint rather than a layer of fibreglass. And so at sea Crowhurst had problems with a boat that cracked and rotted and leaked. Unlike the traditional sailboat, trimarans and catamarans sit on the water rather than in it. There isn't a lot of *digging in* and in storms one runs the constant risk of *pitch poling:* running down a big wave, smashing the bow of the boat into the water and then flipping over, just like pole vaulting only you go upside down. And you die—a major fear of Crowhurst's. But a bigger fear was telling the truth.

me

It's after midnight and the boat rocks and rocks. I'm in a flannel nightie, combat boots and a leather jacket. The small heater provides no heat but a constant whir that muffles the outside, just like my mind, I think.

Crowhurst

Crowhurst was no dummy. It didn't take long for him to figure out that he could never complete the journey. But Crowhurst had banked everything on winning. His business in England, *Electron Utilisation,* was failing. This was his chance to turn it all around. Prize money, publicity, all the opportunities that would await the winner. So he pretended. He never left the Atlantic and radioed in a fake course with vague positions. He kept a phony logbook and planned a rendezvous with himself when the phantom *Teignmouth Electron* sailed back into the Atlantic. Placing second or third would mean his logbooks wouldn't receive the same brutal scrutiny first place would bring. If he could carry it off.

The romantic Frenchman, Bernard Moitessier, was in the lead, sailing without a two-way radio—it destroyed the purity of solo sailing. In letters fired from a slingshot to passing boats, Moitessier explained that he had decided, after rounding Cape Horn, that life in Europe was insane. He had no desire to return and headed to the South Pacific to spend three years on a remote atoll in the Tuamotu Archipelago.

Now, while people were busy debating the apparent madness of Moitessier, Donald Crowhurst was really going nuts. With Moitessier following his heart, Crowhurst was now neck and neck with Tetley, another British sailor, who was driving his boat into the waves trying to catch up to the imaginary position of Crowhurst. Tetley strained his boat too far and sank, sitting in a dinghy at midnight, awaiting rescue.

m e

2 A.M. I've been on deck four times now. The wind has come up and the boat is rocking. I try to sleep but the hideous shape of the lantern swaying sends me stomping up on deck, convinced we are adrift. Still at the wharf. Shining the flashlight around, I scan for perverts. Relief. The light of the neighbours still burns. I'm not really alone. So I creep off the *Snapper* and sneak up to the side of their boat. Just need to see another human, even one asleep. It's a nightlight. There is no one on board. I'm utterly and completely alone. It's just me and Bob's dreams, bobbing up and down.

Back in the boat, I sit on the bunk. I'm terrified and covered in sweat. I can't sleep because I've realized the boat is lower in the stern than the bow. We are sinking from the stern. I take a glass and put it on the floor. It rolls to the stern. So I rip up the hatch over the engine expecting to see water flowing in but there is nothing. I realize at this point I don't even know how to turn the engine on. So much for escape. I hop back to the bunk, knocking over some books. An envelope falls—a letter, two photos on the floor.

Crowhurst

4 A.M. The fates propelled Crowhurst to the lead. His logbooks show his descent into madness as he realized he would be found out. Reality drove him mad. After developing his own

psychotic, religious-type philosophy in logbook entries concerning mostly *The Game* (which he now understood), Crowhurst began a countdown and made his final entry. Then, accompanied by his broken chronometer, he jumped overboard. So much for Donald Crowhurst. The *Teignmouth Electron* was found floating abandoned on the Atlantic, with the logbooks awaiting inspection. Crowhurst died in his bubble of madness but the truth cruised on, awaiting discovery.

m e

Dawn. As grey light breaks on the horizon, I sigh into the now-gentle wind. I'm on deck, leaning on the mast, smoking a cigarette and wrapped in the sleeping bag. I hold an umbrella up to the soft drizzle. I can jump on the dock if we sink. No perverts can creep down below and surprise me. I can see the horizon. I'm steady. I've been here since 4:15 A.M. I've been sitting on the deck, almost on the dock. But not quite.

They smile in the photos, entwined, soft and blurry in bed, her arms out, holding the camera before them. Tea above the tree line—a ritual I clearly misunderstood.

Standing up, I begin to open the hatch to go below. I'm hooked to the safety line in case of an unanticipated, huge breeze. I unhook. I suddenly realize how this must look, and how things have always looked. The adult forgets what the little kid knew and vows are betrayed until the moment when it's clear, at some stage you can't pinpoint, you began plotting the course of your own sorrow. Morning brings a whole new perspective. I go below. In jeans, I climb back out on deck. I rip up the Back Fat letter and scatter it on the water. And I toss the photos over—they float on the waves.

I see my face in the bus window, dark shadows and curves, a hint of an eye. I touch my finger to the glass, trying to find some centre point from which to pull together the abstractions but I find only the artist's negative space, shadows covered with thumb smudges, then lost in the putrid steam of my sleepless breath.

Polish

Elizabeth Ruth

MOTHER IS POLISHING.

She spreads an old towel across the kitchen table where Grandma Hiller's wedding silver is laid out in an organized fashion, left to right, large knives and serving spoons ending the procession at the far corner. Just like Grandma Hiller did it. Irene's oldest, Dana, is watching. Have to remind myself sometimes that Dana's really nothing more than a baby, pressing up close to eight now, with ears so big they make the rest of her seem deformed. Mother says Dana's the curious one in Irene's lot because of the way her head's cocked to one side most of the time. Like she can't quite make out what you're trying to tell her, or, like she wants to hear some more. Personally, I think Dana's head's tilted 'cause it's pregnant with too much information, information too heavy for that twig of a neck.

"Joanna, why do you have to go meddling, getting yourself tangled up in other people's sheets? Best just to leave them well enough alone." Mother doesn't like me talking to Irene about John, says, what would I know about marriage, anyway. She really wants me to ignore Irene's bruises and the children's steely silence. To pretend this generation of Hillers is different from the last. But I'm not good at looking in a different direction when I see a ten-ton truck barrelling up.

Mother clucks the side of her cheek with her tongue. "Tch. Tch. Tch." Shakes her head slowly. It's the same thing every time she polishes. "This used to be a twelve-piece setting." She sighs, breathing out through her nose like a bull in the ring. "Not a missing one." She looks ready to charge but I just start polishing. It's the same speech before all the major holidays, about how the setting isn't complete, about how somebody won't get all the lumps out of the mashed potatoes, about how I'm still single. It's a wonder she can manage to be so freshly disappointed.

Mother only hauls out the good dishes when the table will be full, like it's some sort of punishment the rest of the time. I do the math. This year we'll be ten, what with John when he finally gets here, Irene and her three, my other sister, Caroline, and her husband, my parents and of course, me.

"Won't need twelve, anyway," I say.

Mother looks irritated.

"Maybe someday soon."

She winks at Dana but we all know it was meant for me.

I don't bother to correct her anymore, mother's got a way of seeing what she wants to see, suppose that's true for everyone. Still, there's no point in me telling her again not to hold her breath. I've got no plans for a wedding. Heck, you won't catch me dead in a regular old dress.

Dana watches closely while mother rubs the blackened cotton cloth between her thumb and forefinger, polishing the concealed spoon like maybe she's got a loaded gun under there and is deciding where to aim it. Every now and then she releases her grip, brings the spoon or fork or ladle up in front of her bifocals and examines it with such intensity that I practically flinch, hit the floor and cover my head from spraying bullets.

"Won't come clean," she tells me. Or, "This one's the darndest."

Dana's observing more intently than usual. Her eyes focus on mother's hands as she tips the can of Brasso, holding the cloth over the hole in one and selecting the next piece of silver with the other. All the while she's polishing and telling stories as if Dana and me aren't even in the room. Most of the time she talks about her mother and her mother before that. When she gets to the part about Grandma Hiller nursing Grandpa Hiller for the last years of his life, Dana sits up straight as an arrow.

"Why?" she asks.

"What do you mean, why?" Mother hates to be interrupted.

"Why'd she do that?" Dana repeats.

That's when mother stops what she's doing and stares at her granddaughter like she's never seen her before. Her hands continue polishing in furious motion, but her voice is slow and sure.

"Because she was his wife."

Dana's forehead wrinkles, making her look older and younger at the same time.

"You mean, like, it was her job?" she says, all matter of fact.

Mother looks sharply in my direction, as if I had something to do with this. Any time one of us Hillers start talking women's rights, expressing our thoughts about marriage and baby-making, or even asking simple questions, mother shoots *me* with the look. It's the look that says, "Oh, so it's not good enough that you're a *man-hater*, you had to be recruiting too!" So, I say nothing. Let Dana form her own opinions. I know right about now mother's thinking to herself, "What a bloody nuisance." Or maybe she isn't sure what to think at all anymore.

"No ... yes ... well, not exactly," she begins. "She loved him, loved your great-grandpa."

Dana's expected to be satisfied now so mother turns her back and sets another shiny spoon on the towel. My niece stares into her lap like she's wet herself but doesn't want to say so. I bet she's wondering about her own parents. About what love can do. Just then, Irene walks into the kitchen.

"What's up? Want some help?" And not waiting for an answer Irene pulls out a chair across from me, starts pinning up her hair and gets ready to polish.

"Well," I say. "We're at the part where Grandma Hiller nursed her sick husband and your daughter's not convinced she was a saint."

"Don't put words in my mouth, Joanna!" mother snaps. "All I said was she loved him for better or— "

"Worse." Irene finishes the sentence and rolls her eyes in my direction.

I can't help smirking. We both remember our grandparents well because we were already teenagers when they died. The giant bowls of sugary strawberries and Grandma Hiller's rolling sausage arms are what I remember best. And her smell. Talcum powder and lavender perfume which she always corrected me and said was toilet water. (Personally, I thought perfume sounded a whole lot prettier.) Anyway, we don't talk about Grandpa Hiller nearly as much, about how his hunting rifle sat propped up against the dining room table, or about the stick no thicker than his thumb, which hung just inside his clothes closet. Or how he answered our grandmother's questions before she had a chance to ask them. No, we never talked about those things. Grandpa Hiller's illness was not the worst of it and just when I'm about to say so, Dana opens her mouth to speak again.

"Do you love Daddy?" she asks Irene directly.

Mother intercepts before Irene has time to pull an answer together. "Pass me that one, Dana," she orders, pointing to a grapefruit spoon.

Dana moves quickly, doing what she's told. She passes the spoon, careful not to catch the tender skin of her fingertips along the serrated edge.

I'm still waiting for Irene to speak as mother presses down into the curve of the utensil with her thumb until it turns purple. Then she works her way up the handle with the same vigour and I roll up my sleeves because suddenly it feels warm in the kitchen.

"Aw, she didn't love him," Irene says, picking up the conversation and putting it down somewhere else. "She didn't really love him. That's not what that's about. Just couldn't say no to the man."

I wink at Irene to show agreement. Think, good for you. Tell it like it is.

Dana's eyes widen with interest, maybe hope, and I swallow hard, wondering what mother's going to do now. I sort of slink back down on my chair because I had nothing to do with that one, although my talk from last year, about Lea, was probably coming to mother's mind just then.

"You're going to be hurt, Joanna," she'd told me. "That woman seduced you and she's evil. This can come to no good." I didn't tell her I'd been living with Lea for seven years by then and that Irene and the kids came to visit from time to time, especially when John lost his temper. Instead, I just dug my fingernails into the palms of my hand and waited until mother was finished ranting.

"Real love," I told her calmly, "doesn't hurt."

Now, today, in the kitchen, I'm feeling that same kind of tension, hearing Irene speaking the truth even when it gets under mother's skin—well, especially then. Irene tugs on Dana's ponytail and tells her to never mind and go find her brother and sister. She screeches her chair across the new linoleum, which causes mother to clench her teeth, and then Dana bolts from the room.

Mother's quick to check under the chair for marks on the floor. "Teach that child some manners, eh?" she says, more telling than asking.

Irene looks at me with a stone-cold expression, probably the one she thinks mother deserves but can't quite muster the courage to deliver. "I don't want my girls filled with that garbage," she hisses at mother.

Right then there's a long silence and in that long silence

I wish we could fast forward to the part in mother's story where Dad left fish hanging under the dock at Tobermory and an otter ate all of them. Or when she had to deliver Caroline by herself on the kitchen table, cut the baby away from her with a paring knife because she was being strangled by her own umbilical cord. But, mother never skips through time like that. We have to get there chronologically, or not at all.

Now suddenly she's frantic, arranging and rearranging silver.

"The pickle fork!" she squeals. "It's missing!"

Irene and I pick up new polishing cloths, no point in going further with that line of talk. Mother's notions about the family are as sanitized and orderly as the silver we eat from; and also missing a few key pieces. Like the fact that her grandfather, like her own father and like Irene's John, were all big drinkers. Carried bottles of scotch in their inside breast pockets, liked their women in dresses—no makeup—always cleaning up their images in front of town. No need to say it out loud, though. We all know the truth. Love was the main thing missing.

Mother leans against the counter, her right arm hanging limp at her side, bewildered. "Where on earth could it be?"

Irene stares a hard one right at me, as if to say, "You haven't seen it have you, Joanna?" I ignore her and just keep on polishing. But when I look up not a minute later, feeling a hot spot bore through my cheek, I find my smart-ass sister still staring at me with a broad smile and eyes big and stupid like a cow's. I'm pretty sure she knows something. When I get up to wash my hands with dish soap, the phone rings. Irene answers.

"Hello?"

Pause.

"John? That you?"

Pause.

"Do we have to go over this again?" Irene's voice is impatient, irritated, and it kind of surprises me because this is not how my sister sounds when her husband's within reach of her. Mother puts down her last piece of silver and inspects Irene. "You heard me," Irene continues, even louder than before. "And this time, I'm not changing my mind."

I don't turn around to face her. My heart is pumping thunder in my chest but Irene sounds serious, like a person does when they've finally made a hard decision. Instead, I hold my breath and cross my fingers in the sink where she and mother won't see. *Come on, Sis,* I think. *You can do it.* I want to hear her scream into the phone, tell John exactly what he deserves, but Irene sounds more like all the screaming days are over. I wish *I* could forgive and forget. But it was just last year when I learned how bad things had got, just before Thanksgiving then too.

In the middle of the night, Irene was yelling and crying mostly, and John, being his worst self, was taking in more oxygen than should be permitted one human being, sucking the life out of everyone around him.

"Bitch!" he'd called Irene. "Ugly useless bitch."

Nobody in the house moved, but I was laying in bed, screaming into my pillow for my sister, by proxy. A while later, when it got dead again, I wandered down to the kitchen. Mother had already set out the following day's preparations. Vegetables were in the rinsing sink. A pot of water on a back burner of the stove was filled with twenty pounds of peeled Prince Edward Island potatoes. Two turnips still in their thick waxy coats, and a bag of fresh cranberries to be cooked were on the counter. Four loaves of bread, pulled apart and seasoned for dressing sat in covered pans ready for Dad to stuff the bird with before it went into the oven.

I was desert-thirsty and pretty sure there would be at least three cans of apple juice sitting on the top shelf of the fridge. Mother shops in bulk when company's expected. The only thing I couldn't locate was the can opener. Not in the knife drawer. Not in the dishwasher. Caroline and Henry were asleep in the den off the kitchen and I didn't want to disturb them with the lights, so instead I rummaged through the army of foodstuffs on the table. Still, no can opener. But then, there, shining in the darkness like the Aurora Borealis, was mother's sharp-pronged pickle fork. I grabbed it up and swiftly ruptured the thin lid of the apple juice can like I was poking into John's beer gut. Punishing him. I also broke the fork.

Realizing what I'd done, and remembering the conversation I'd had that afternoon with mother about Lea and me, I suddenly panicked. It was like everything unspoken in our family came rushing back to me in a flood and I'd carelessly, selfishly, lost the plug that could stop it. So, in my green pinstriped pajamas and bare feet, I ran out through the pantry, into the backyard, my blood racing something fierce. What did I do? What's wrong with me? What if I was cursed for being the first to destroy something irreplaceable? *Tradition.*

Out in the backyard I feverishly dug under the porch like a dog digging for a bone. The strange thing was—and I still don't know why this happened—I stopped caring about what mother thought anymore. I thought about Irene and her marriage. And Grandma Hiller's. While I was digging I thought about habits that get formed over time, like having to eat with the same silver every holiday, or having to settle for what you're used to—like marriage—or not knowing how to say "no." And while I was thinking and digging, I remembered the look on Grandma Hiller's face at my grandfather's funeral. She watched men throw dirt over the coffin like she couldn't believe he was mortal after all. I asked mother about it later and she said poor Grandma Hiller, dear sweet Grandma Hiller, hadn't been able to tear herself away, hadn't been able to accept the loss. All of a sudden, on my hands and knees in the backyard, tears pouring out of me like bitter wine, I was sure that my grandmother had been standing so still in order to make sure her husband was really gone, but good.

That's when I dropped the pickle fork into the hole, covered it in soil, and replaced the stone. Then I sat in the dark of the country night, cool mist of morning dew kissing my toes. It seemed right, that's all. And, as I got up and turned to go back into the house the curtains in Irene's room moved just a little. Maybe it was the wind, I thought. But then again, maybe Grandma Hiller was trying to tell me something.

Now, this afternoon, while Irene's saying goodbye to John on the phone, I can see that exact spot, out the kitchen window. Mother's still on her hands and knees, her head buried inside the buffet, like an ostrich with its head in the sand. She's still hoping to find the fork. Irene still sounds final.

"No, John," she says. "It's dead." Then she quietly hangs up.

I reach into the drawer for a clean dishtowel, wipe my hands and look Irene straight in the eyes. She doesn't turn away, as if looking anywhere else might change her mind. Like she might pick up the receiver again and press redial. You can do this, I think to myself. You can. Just then, mother pokes her head out from the buffet.

"Things all right with John," she says, half asking, half insisting.

My sister says nothing.

I clench my fists, feeling like someone in this family has got to stick to their guns. I imagine Lea's sweet face and our home together. Then I hold my breath again, the way Dana does for good luck, when we're driving past the cemetery.

Mother addresses Irene again, expectantly. "John's on his way, right?"

I'm still clinging to Irene with my lifeboat eyes when a grin spreads across her face, this time the smartest one I've seen in years.

"No, mother," she says, winking at me. "No."

Mermaids

Kelly Watt

IT IS LATE in the day. An aging orange sun hovers above the lake. The girl lies on her belly by the edge of the pool, hypnotized by the dance of chlorine, marvelling at the ability of water to shrink limbs. She puts her small hand in the water, then quickly pulls it out again.

"It's a dwarf hand," she says out loud.

In the middle of her play, she hears a splash from the deep end. Something moves underwater. It is pink and orange and flutters like seaweed. What could it be? She looks up to see if anyone else has seen. An old man dozes in a chaise lounge. Shadows creep along the deck. Forgotten beach towels lie in soggy lumps. Somewhere, someone has left a transistor on. At noon the pool was crowded. Now almost everyone has gone for dinner. Except for the girl and her mother, the old man and two women at the far end. Two mothers. They sit surrounded by pool toys. They laugh and play crazy eights.

The girl is on holiday with her mother, but without her father. Her mother won't say where her father went. The girl is not supposed to ask so many questions. Her mother got cross with her about that very thing this morning. When he first went away her mother said he had gone on a little trip. But now they're on a little trip and he isn't with them. Every morning the girl gets up early and rushes down to the dining room looking for him, as if to catch him lurking among the cornflakes.

They are staying at a resort called Gray Rocks Inn. Everything has a French name like on cartons of milk. There are heads of animals on the walls. Their eyes follow the girl wherever she goes, even though they're dead.

There is also a trampoline and water-skiing and golfing. All the other kids go golfing in the mornings and get a prize even if they're no good. But the girl doesn't want to play golf. She is afraid to let her mother out of her sight in case she goes missing too. Her mother is annoyed about this.

"You are always underfoot," she complains. "You're sticking like glue. Give me some space!"

The girl's mother is tanned. She wears a swimsuit but never swims. She drinks gin and tonics and smokes Rothmans cigarettes. In the afternoons she experiments with new hairstyles. She has dyed her hair twice since they came to the lake. The girl thinks the colours have names like ice cream flavours. Today her mother's hair is strawberry. She is wearing sunglasses and reading a ladies' magazine. She holds a chewed pencil in her hand. Occasionally she reads the questions out loud.

"Are you his dream wife?" she reads. "Do you greet him

at the door every day with a smile? Fat lot of help that is," her mother snorts and scribbles furiously in the margins.

In the mornings, her mother won't get out of bed. She lies among the sheets twirling her hair into blond question marks that stick to her head. She stares at the ceiling scowling and smoking cigarettes. Every day the girl asks when her father is coming back.

"I don't know!" her mother yells. They had a fight about this an hour ago. Her mother is still not talking and the girl sulks and talks to herself. Every day at lunch her mother offers her a quarter if she can make it through a meal without talking. But the girl never makes it to dessert.

"I see something," the girl says now. She has given up on the silent treatment and wants a truce.

"Stop bothering me," her mother says.

The sun sinks another inch and the shade creeps forward, claiming new territory on the deck. The old man gets up and walks slowly away. Even his toes are wrinkled. The girl slips her hand under water.

"Into the water you go," she says. She examines her shrunken hand, the mysterious water. Again she sees something. It flutters like seaweed, gently sinking toward the pool's blue bottom. No one else is in the pool. It is her little secret.

She has other secrets too. She knows her mother goes out at night when she thinks the girl is asleep. Her mother sits in the bar and laughs with strange men. When she comes home she smells of gin and cigarettes. If her mother sneaks off during the day, the girl always finds her there. Sometimes the girl goes into the bar to look for her mother. The bartender's name is Hal and he gives her Shirley Temples on the house. All the men give her their swizzle sticks. She has been here nearly a week and already has sixty-six. She rents them out for five cents a stir. When she goes home she is going to sell them. Buy a train ticket to wherever her daddy is.

In the deep end, she sees the candy-coloured seaweed again. "Mermaid," the girl says. She sticks her hand under water, waves her dwarf hand at it.

"I see you," she says.

"What?" her mother asks.

"Nothing."

"What are you doing?"

"There's a mermaid," the girl says.

"Nonsense," her mother snaps.

Mermaids are lucky, the girl thinks. She doesn't really believe in mermaids, but likes to pretend. She and her daddy play pretend in the pool at Sunnyside. He is a sea horse and she is the mermaid. She rides on his shoulders round and round the deep end. They play this in the bath together too. She sits on his lap and he jumps her up and down, saying whoops-a-daisy! Her mother broke dishes when she found them together in the bath naked. At least her daddy doesn't sit on a chaise lounge all day tanning and smoking cigarettes.

The girl plunks her feet into the water.

"Dwarf feet," she says.

The mermaid responds. Her seaweed hair spins, revealing a desperate-moon face, her pink and orange body a flurry of limbs.

The girl rests her elbows on her knees, her chin in her hands. She talks to her new friend. She tells the mermaid she's on vacation with her mother. That her daddy didn't come. That she doesn't know where he is and her mother won't go swimming. The mermaid groans, a bubble escaping like a scream from the silent O of her mouth. The girl's mother sighs and slaps the magazine onto her legs.

"I miss my daddy," the girl whines. "It's not the same. Nothing is the same without my daddy. I want my daddy," she says. The mermaid disappears under a torrent of splashing.

"I WANT MY DADDY, I WANT MY DADDY, I WANT MY DADDY," the girl shrieks. The women look up briefly from their game of crazy eights.

The girl's mother closes her eyes. She picks up her wasting gin and tonic and sucks the last drops through the straw, making a noise she would scold the girl for making. She gets up from her chair, goes over and slaps the girl.

"He's not coming, okay? He's not coming today, he's not coming tomorrow, daddy's not coming back ever. He was no good. Are you happy now? You've ruined everything!" She stomps back to her chaise lounge and buries her face in her magazine. The girl cries quietly, the tears falling onto her wet hands.

On the other side of the pool, one of the card playing mothers glances around the patio with a worried face. She calls: "Darlene!" but Darlene doesn't come. The transistor croons softly. Over it can be heard the gentle slapping noises of water, from the pool, the lake. There is the drone of a motorboat crossing the bay.

In the deep end, an abandoned plastic fish rocks gently.

The girl picks a scab on her knee. "I hate you," she says to no one in particular. A stream of bubbles erupts from the pool's blue depths. The girl's mother lights a cigarette and counts out loud to ten.

Darlene's mother puts down her cards and says so long to her friend. She folds her beach towel and puts it in her basket. She waves goodbye and walks slowly, a hand to her brow, surveying the pool, the sandbox, the beach. She wears flip flops and a yellow sun dress. She calls softly, "Darlene?"

The sun slips into the lake, a memory of orange. The deck is chill. The mermaid bumps along the pool's blue bottom and is still.

"I see you," the girl says.

The Girl with the Blue Hat (An Urban Fable)

Teresa McWhirter

THE GIRL WITH THE BLUE hat loved a boy named Oliver. They lived together in a house with a garden. She liked to make pies and cakes and Oliver liked to cook spaghetti. They didn't have much money but he made a great tomato sauce.

The furniture in their house had been found abandoned at garage sales. They bought an old lamp and Oliver painted the shade with daisies. She once brought home a ceramic hula girl. Oliver painted that, too.

Oliver also painted large canvasses with angels on them. The angels were always girls and they were always beautiful. The girl with the blue hat was happy in their little home.

Then it happened that Oliver began painting angels that were not as beautiful, that had long teeth and tangled hair. The girl knew they were still angels though, she could tell by the wings. One day she came home and Oliver was packing a suitcase. "Where are you going?" she asked.

"Away," Oliver said.

She got a slice of cherry pie and sat at the table. The pie didn't taste so good, but she ate it anyway. When she was done she washed her plate and drank a glass of water. Oliver finished packing.

"Are you coming back?" she asked. She spread her hands across the table and waited for him to answer. Her fingers were very short and the nails badly bitten. She didn't like looking at her hands so she looked at Oliver.

"I do not love you," Oliver said. He stood at the door in his baggy green sweater. Oliver's fingers were long and beautiful. He used them to brush the hair out of his eyes. "I'm sorry," he said, "but I'm not the person you thought."

Oliver opened the door and left. The girl sat still for a long time. Oliver had not taken his angel paintings, which she stacked and took to the backyard. She made a circle with rocks from the garden and burned each canvas. Then she continued to remove the traces of Oliver from her life. She took his name from the mailbox. She changed the answering machine message. She cleared out his remaining clothes and shoes and put them in a Hefty bag on the curb. Boxes of spaghetti were thrown out. She tore up her basil and oregano plants. She put Oliver's pictures and poems into a shoe box, which she stored in the bottom of the closet. Later when she was looking for a sweater she saw the box, so she buried it in the garden beside the missing herb plants.

A long time passed and still she could not forget Oliver. She juxtaposed herself in different moments. Maybe he didn't like pies, maybe he never had. She wondered what Oliver thought as he painted and puttered in the garden or slept beside her. *I do not love you,* he'd said. What Oliver had not said was, *anymore.*

The girl with the blue hat stayed in the house where she and Oliver had lived. She liked the organized cupboards and the way the light crept through the window shades. Sometimes she would see Oliver's friends downtown. They said he had left the city but she didn't ask where. Eventually she stopped going places where she would see people they knew. Reasons for Oliver's departure seemed as extraneous as her diaphragm or their family pass to the museum.

The girl with the blue hat planned out perfect funerals for Oliver. She imagined herself in an elegant black dress and a veil or sometimes a pink dress and a large pink hat. On very lonely nights she wrapped her arms around the pillow and pretended it was Oliver. She still made cakes and pies, but could rarely eat them. They grew mouldy on the counter and she put them in the compost heap. Then she made more.

When winter came the girl with the blue hat heard a snow warning and imagined her and Oliver trapped in their little house with no electricity. She put candles and a flashlight and extra batteries in the cupboard beside the sink.

Many things changed. She skipped the pasta aisle at the grocery store. She did not listen to the radio in case she heard a love song. She no longer enjoyed reading art books. Oliver laid claim to many things. Sometimes she was angry at Oliver, but it was hard to hate a ghost.

The girl with the blue hat found it easier not to get up. She slept in a sleeping bag on the futon couch because the real bed still smelled like Oliver, even though she had replaced the sheets and pillowcases. She left the lights off more and more because she did not want to see the white spots on the wall where his canvasses used to hang. She stopped making pies and cakes. She stopped eating tomato sauce and onions. The girl with the blue hat grew very thin.

One day she realized she could no longer afford to live in the house. She didn't know where to go and didn't want to leave the garden. In the kitchen she took out the knife she used to peel apples and made a mark on her chest over her heart. She wanted to wrap her heart in plastic and leave it on the counter for Oliver, in case he ever came back.

When the girl with the blue hat got out of the hospital she moved into an apartment. She did not have a garden. After a while she began to make loaves of bread: rye, whole wheat, olive loaf. Bread was healthier than pies and she found it lasted much longer.

Eventually the girl with the blue hat began to go downtown. She did not see Oliver's friends anymore. She started to go out at night to bars where the music was very loud. At night she was never afraid to walk down the streets alone.

One night a boy came home with her. He wanted to sleep over and she said all right. By then the girl with the blue hat had a new bed. She did not tell the boy about the months spent sleeping on the couch. She didn't tell him much of anything.

Many boys began to sleep over. She didn't mind. Sometimes they stayed for days. Sometimes they said they loved her. Then the girl with the blue hat would disappear. It was easy to be a ghost, just as she expected.

The Writers

Dana Bath

Dana Bath has won prizes from *Grain* magazine's Short Grain Contest (First Prize for Postcard Fiction 1999), Anvil Press's International Three-Day Novel Contest (Third Prize 1998, Second Prize 1999), and *This* Magazine's Great Canadian Literary Hunt (Honourable Mention 1998). She has published fiction in *Index, A Room of One's Own, Grain, sub-Terrain* and *Matrix* magazines. She has also published nonfiction in *Bitch, Matrix, Index* and *Hour Montreal*. Her book of short stories, *What Might Have Been Rain,* was published in 1998 and her first novel, *Plenty of Harm in God,* was released in 2001.

Originally from Corner Brook, Newfoundland, Bath has lived, studied and worked around Canada, Europe and Asia and now lives in Montreal, where she teaches college English and is at work on a second novel. Bath received her MA in English and Creative Writing from Concordia University in 2000.

Heather Birrell

Heather Birrell's work has appeared in *The Journey Prize Anthology, Prism International* and *The New Quarterly*. Birrell is a fellow of the MacDowell Colony in New Hampshire and Fundacion Valparaiso in Spain.

Birrell lives, writes and teaches in Toronto. She is at work on a collection of short stories.

Natalee Caple

Natalee Caple's fiction has been nominated for a National Magazine Award, the Journey Prize, the Bronwen Wallace Award and the Eden Mills Fiction Award. Her stories and poems have appeared in *Descant, The Malahat Review, Blood & Aphorisms* and many other journals and magazines. Caple is the author of three books, *The Plight of Happy People in an Ordinary World,* a novel; *The Heart Is its Own Reason,* a collection of short stories; and *A More Tender Ocean,* a book of poetry. Caple also co-edited *The Notebooks* with Michelle Berry, an anthology of interviews with and short fiction by seventeen contemporary writers.

Born in Montreal, Caple resides in Toronto where she is the literary editor of *The Queen Street Quarterly.*

Christy Ann Conlin

Christy Ann Conlin's writing and photography have appeared in various publications including *This* Magazine, *The Vancouver Sun, Chatelaine, Saturday Night* Magazine and *The Coast.* Conlin's first novel, *Heave,* was released in 2002.

Born and raised in the Annapolis Valley, Nova Scotia, Conlin has worked as a seasonal fruit picker, a factory worker, a teacher, a researcher and a science-grant writer. She has travelled and lived in the U.S., Korea and Europe and she recently spent time as a storytelling apprentice in Ireland. Conlin now resides in Nova Scotia.

Kristen den Hartog

Kristen den Hartog's short stories have appeared in numerous publications including *The Journey Prize Anthology* (1997) and *Turn of the Story: Canadian Short Fiction on the Eve of the Millennium.* Her first novel, *Water Wings,* was released in 2001 and her second novel, *The Perpetual Ending,* is due to be released early in 2003.

Born in Deep River, Ontario, she now resides in Toronto.

Annabel Lyon

Annabel Lyon's stories have appeared in numerous journals and anthologies, including the *Journey Prize Anthology* (2000) and *Toronto Life* Magazine. Lyon's journalism has appeared in *The Vancouver Sun,* the *Ottawa Citizen* and the *National Post.* Her first book, *Oxygen,* a collection of short fiction, was released in 2000. Her second book, a novel, is to be published in spring 2003.

Lyon has a degree in philosophy from Simon Fraser University and an MFA in creative writing from the University of British Columbia. She lives in Vancouver.

Suzanne Matczuk

Suzanne Matczuk won the distinction of most promising Manitoba writer at the Manitoba Book Awards 2002. She has also won a National Magazine Award and an Atlantic Journalism Award. She is the author of *Cocktail-O-matic: The Little Black Book of Cocktail,* an historic account of all things related to drink.

Matczuk is a freelance writer and broadcaster. She has worked as a producer for CBC radio and written for a number of magazines and newspapers including *The Globe and Mail* and the *National Post.* "Book of Lies" is based on characters from a historical novel Matczuk is currently working on. She lives in Winnipeg.

Teresa McWhirter

Teresa McWhirter's work has been published in *Geist, Vice, Bust, sub-Terrain* and *The Capilano Review.* Her first book, *Some Girls Do,* was published in May 2002.

McWhirter was born in Vancouver and grew up in Kimberley, B.C. A graduate of the University of Victoria's creative writing program, she now lives on Vancouver's east side.

Elizabeth Ruth

Elizabeth Ruth's first novel, *Ten Good Seconds of Silence*, was shortlisted for the 2001 Roger's Writers' Trust of Canada Fiction Prize and the Amazon.com/Chapters/Books in Canada First Novel Award 2001. Her short fiction has been published in literary journals across Canada. She has also written for CBC radio and for film. Ruth is the editor of the 2002 anthology, *Bent on Writing*.

Born in Windsor, Ontario, Ruth now resides in Toronto where she is an editor with *Fireweed Feminist Quarterly*, teaches short story writing at George Brown College and writes book reviews for *The Globe and Mail*. Ruth is also working on a new novel.

Kelly Watt

Kelly Watt's short fiction has been published in literary journals across the country and her first novel, *Mad Dog*, was published in 2001. Watt grew up in Toronto and has lived and travelled in India, Nepal, France and England. She has worked in journalism and publishing.

Watt is now at work on her second novel and lives (and gardens) with her husband and dog just outside of Toronto.